Mormon Cowboy

To David B. Jenninim

Happy Travels

MORMON COWBOY

Real Cowboy Stories! Filled with humor, wisdom, adventure, and Western Lore!

Written by a Cowboy
To His Cowboy Dad,
About Their Cowboy
Great-Great-Great Granddad

J.R. "Buster" Thompson

iUniverse, Inc.
New York Lincoln Shanghai

Mormon Cowboy

Real Cowboy Stories! Filled with humor, wisdom, adventure, and
Western Lore!

iUniverse, Inc.

For information address:
iUniverse, Inc.
2021 Pine Lake Road, Suite 100
Lincoln, NE 68512
www.iuniverse.com

This book is a work of fiction. Any resemblance to any persons living or dead
is coincidence.

ISBN: 0-595-31096-6

Printed in the United States of America

Special Thanks:

To my Dad, who is the inspiration for the main character, was know as "Narrow Gauge" by his feller workmen, can fix prêt near anything and displays the adaptive nature of all true Cowboys.

To Mom, who has always encouraged me to write and loves everything I have scratched my name to.

To my wife, who is from Pennsylvania, is Western dyslexic, wears purple Cowboy boots to fend off real Cowboys, thinks "spinning a yarn" is the first step in making a sweater, and will never read this book because she hasn't learned the language.

To my daughter, who asks me not to talk "Cowboy talk" around her friends. So, be'n respectful a her wishes, I don't.

And to my mother-in-law, who was raised in Philadelphia, but has watched every Western, what ever been watched.

—J.R. Buster Thompson

CONTENTS

▼

Excerpts...

From Chapter 1 Nose

"...none of us ever asked him what he used to be called since it was a pretty sore subject for him to talk about."

From Chapter 4 Dying For Your Beliefs

"Folks say that them kids back East in them clean clothes and fancy hats had been reading about how exciting the West was, and that there wasn't nothing but brave men and stalwart women out there a taming the untamed...why this wasn't no more based on fact than a buffalo can fly."

From Chapter 7 Cowboys are Thinkers

"The actual thing of it is, that a Cowboy is one of God's few creatures what spends most of his life just sitting and thinking."

From Chapter 11 God's Pay

"It's times like these when a Cowboy kind of figures God Hisself just needs some entertaining."

Chapter 12 Hop'n and Poke'n"

Cowboy'n is a profession what ain't appreciated for its value unless you been one.

Introduction

These is some a them stories what is wrote to be read out loud. And some of what is in here, just don't make no sense except for if you got a sprig a alfalfa a hanging twixt your teeth, a pair a worn down Cowboy boots on your feet, and the smell of leather or horses somewhere near by.

And if that ain't enough, it'd also be right smart, if who ever is to do the reading, to do her slow enough so as to leave listeners a respectful amount a room for thinking on what's just been read.

You see, good yarns is made better when folks has time to ponder on them for a spell.

And if there's a tear to be shed, or a chuckle to be chuckled, or even a memory to be remembered, it just wouldn't be right if there ain't no time given for shedding, chuckling or remembering.

Now these here yarns only got about a ounce of truth in each. But then, that's kind of how things are remembered most the time anyway.

But they've also got some folks in them who you might think you knew, or even been related to like N. Bateman who was a local Mayor and grain peddler. G. Mouritsen whose profession ain't talked about when women are around. Port who ran the Trading Post. Ned the town drunk. Doc Sorenson and his side kick Doc Dayton. E. Giles who invents milking machines. K. Smith who changes the course of what farmers wear due to a simple problem he is sick and tired of being sick and tired over. And many others.

Just take the main character…feller by the name of Narrow Gauge. He might have been your Dad or granddad. Or even parts of what he done might have been done by your great, great, great granddad.

Well, we got some Cowboy'n to be done, so let's get started.

CHAPTER 1

▼

NOSE

Fifteen days out of Durango and them high-mountain passes. Narrow Gauge and his boys was nigh unto halfway down to Abilene's July rail header, when the winds whipped back, pushed their brims straight up, and commenced to gag them with their own kerchiefs.

This here wind was mighty unusual, since it was a coming hard from the East right in to the faces of their stock, pushing their ponies heads down and leaving the boys unprotected. They found themselves chewing grit and biting dust so thick that the grub cookie was about to add water and make some gravy.

That was if he would have had some water.

There hadn't been moisture on this part of the prairie for nearly a month and they was pushing up what was left of the hard pan the sun had beat down ever since. These here Cowboys had used up the last of their water barrel yesterday and them cows had been a couple of days without a drink,

They hoped there'd be some wet down here. But the mirages had held true and they was now just moving forward with the herd, with hope their noses would bring them to something.

That was until the wind reversed on them and now had them prêt near moving in place. They knew they was bucking it when they got closer and closer to the grub wagon which Nose usually kept out a couple of miles in front so as not to get the grub all contaminated with dust and smell from the herd.

Yep, that wagon was being pushed back by the wind harder than them two mules could pull it along. And a Cowboy could tell they didn't like it much neither. They had them long ears pinned back and their eyes squinted until they was nearly shut. And they had had their tongues hanging out and back for a long time and was totally coated in dust. Looked like they was about to be turned into permanent mule jerky.

The Cowboys had gained on them and the lead punchers had fallen in behind the wagon as to try and take some cover from the wind. They thought they was still moving, but then they heard Nose yell down, "Why don't you get down off of them nags so they don't die with you sorry cowpunchers on them? Least wise we might be able to save the saddles!"

Narrow and the boys looked up, and sure enough, they wasn't moving and neither was the wagon. Narrow looked up at Nose and said, "Maybe this Eastern will bring in a rain. Now the herd's stopped maybe the dust will settle and give us a chance to smell the wind."

Nose said, "Well you better get up here in the front of the wagon. You know, if there's smelling to be done, I ain't going to be the one to do her."

Nose got his name from ain't having had one for the past seven years.

You see, he'd been the best Apache tracker in the Cavalry. His Ma being Apache had helped some. But his real skill had come from his great smelling ability back when he had a nose.

Most trackers knew how to sniff out horse leavings, good ones could even smell where horses had been without the leavings. But Nose had some kind of bloodhound ability where he could sniff around where the Apaches had attacked, even if they had burned every thing to the ground like they usually did. And then he could sniff out the exact same Apaches what had done the deed.

Well, he was in demand by every Cavalry unit from the Great Basin down through parts of the badlands. And for the most part, the Apaches didn't mind much neither because it was the renegades what was doing the burning and raping. The stand-up Apaches was trying to mend their ways with the whites, because they needed the gun trading for hunting.

Anyway, Nose was between assignments on his way up to Silverton where he figured he'd spend a summer in them cool mountain canyons doing a little gambling with the silver miners, and maybe even settling in with one of them miner's daughters (or wives for that matter). He'd saved most of what the Cavalry had paid him and didn't really need for hard currency.

Well, he was picking his way through the aspen up near what they now call Show Low, in the high valley of Northern Arizona Territory, with the breeze coming into his face. When suddenly 'n Apache arrow whistles by his ear and plugs into the quaking aspen right up in front of him.

This arrow was still right at eye level and at a slight upward angle, so who ever had let it fly was on foot, and not more than forty feet behind him.

All this really meant was that if he was supposed to be dead, he would have been already. And any stupid move now would make him dead before he hit the ground. So he just moved on up in his saddle far enough to grab the arrow and pulled it out of the tree from which it was stuck. He then held it out to his side, still not turning and still not moving.

He could smell a couple of braves coming in from the front, and knew he was in for some kind of confrontation with some unfriendlies.

Before he knew it, they were on him, four of them. One was holding his riding horse, one holding his pack pony, and the other two on each side of him. They was renegades all right, and he could also smell some sense of there being more beyond his line of sight.

Renegade Apaches wasn't no different than outlaw whites. They was smart enough to watch their backsides, and if they was about to do something different they would have it pretty well planned out. This wasn't about to be no exception.

The renegade on the right of him motioned for him to dismount. This was a favorite Injun trick, them knowing that white men always mounted and dismounted from the left.

Nose slowly slid hisself down, still holding that arrow in his right hand, and not dare moving his left hand. He didn't hold them up like a white man would when surrendering to another white man. He just kind of held them out, so as to let the Apaches know he wasn't about to try nothing.

The two warriors not tending to his pony's motioned him over in the clearing, took his pistol, long knife and leg knife and threw them down out of reach. They took the Apache arrow he was holding and owl-hooted a signal.

In rode what was to be the renegade leader who was off his pony and quicker than he could wet his lips, up to Nose, face to face.

Nose was scared, but dared not show it because he knew they had some kind of respect for him or they'd a killed him by now.

It's amazing how quiet the woods can get when a handful of Apaches is about to make 'n impression on a white man.

But it was over quick and for that Nose could be mighty grateful.

Before he knew it, the renegade in charge had grabbed Nose by the nose and sliced it clean from his face, mounted his pony and he and the rest of them was gone quicker than the shadow of a shooting star on a clear night. At least wise that's how Nose tells it.

Anyway, that pretty much ended Nose's smelling and scouting career. And didn't do much for him when it came to attracting no miner's daughters nor wives neither.

Story goes…that renegade was scared to kill Nose, because then he'd have the stand-up Apaches after him as well as the US Cavalry.

But he sure didn't need Nose tracking him neither. So he figured he could accomplish what he needed without no severe bloodshed by just carving off that nose. He didn't last long though, because between him and the other Apaches with him, the next time they got a little fire water in them they was bragging up their dirty deed to the other competing renegades, and sure enough the competing renegades killed him just to get that there nose for their own leader's belt.

Well, this went on for pretty much a whole year until most of the renegades had killed each other off just for the privilege of owning that stupid nose. So there wasn't many renegades for Nose left to track even if he would have had his nose still on his face.

Some folks say it was just destiny that nose was going to take care of the worst Apaches anyway, whether Nose was sniffing through it or not.

Anyway, that's how Nose got his name and none of us ever asked him what he used to be called since it was a pretty sore subject for him to talk about.

Since his face healed up he'd been running a pretty good grub wagon for the cattle pushers what needed one, in spite of the fact that he couldn't smell what he cooked. But then there wasn't much bad he could do to beans, bacon, biscuits and gravy. Of course every now and again, we'd have to butcher one of the cattle due to a broke leg, and he'd spiked the whole thing for us. But it didn't take much smelling to tell when it was time to carve it up.

But here Narrow was, climbing up through the wagon to the front to see if he could catch a whiff of any smell of on-coming rain. He couldn't, but the time it took to do it kind of took the edge off the desperation he was feeling.

The dust and wind had been so strong that the boys hadn't realized it was dusk and time to settle the herd in. But no sooner rode the perimeter and drove in the stragglers than the coyotes went quiet and a huge thunderclap brought all those sorry heads up. A cloud burst came down on this gaggle a hoofs horns and hats like God Hisself had decided to see how many cows He could drown. But this wasn't no ordinary cloudburst. This here storm lasted through the entire night, filled Nose's chuck wagon rain barrel and filled every low spot as far as they could ride for the next day or two.

The drink was good, but the smell of wet cows, horses and dirty Cowboys close to choked them to death.

That is except for Nose, who couldn't of noticed if he'd been rammed head first up the wrong end of the sickest calf in the herd.

Anyway, the Cowboys was back on the trail again, and ain't got no more than the usual complaints.

CHAPTER 2

▼

GREENBEAN

Owing to the fact that neither Narrow Gauge ner none of the other boys had seen him push in through the swinging doors, didn't keep the smoky air from changing. Even Billy eventually stopped his piano playing, giving way to a silence that any preacher would of wanted in his pews on a Sunday morning.

Like most misunderstandings this one was based more on fiction than fact.

You see, Narrow Gauge had just moved his entire crew from the Columbine spread up to the Golden Horseshoe. He had taken the come-on-over money he and the boys got up front and they had headed over the pass for a weekend of trouble-making with the local easy women over in Silverton.

This wasn't nothing unusual except for on the way up over the mountain, Narrow's boys started tipping the bottle early and was feeling better than they should have been, when their ponies brought them into town late that Saturday night. Narrow hisself wasn't no drinker, and no womanizer for that matter, having been raised in a non-drinking Mormon family. But he figured as Foreman of this crew, it was his duty to keep his boys in line. And in order to do that, he had to be watching over them prêt near every minute they wasn't pushing cows.

By this time of night, both saloons was pretty much filled up with local miners, high mountain trappers come in for their weekly baths and booze, and many of the legitimate folk what didn't have no reputations to keep.

In Silverton things was pretty much available to those what wanted them. Gambling, drinking, Billy's bad piano playing and womanizing for them what could fight there way to the front of the line for the few women what wanted to be womanized.

Contrary to what most had heard about Silverton, there wasn't much shooting. Folks pretty much respected each other and left their guns holstered if they had them. 'Course that's something else that most people didn't appreciate. That is to say, there wasn't many folks that actually walked around with shooting irons strapped to their sides. Mostly those that did was either just passing through town or they was a prospector that had just stumbled into a big paycheck and spent it all on a new sidearm and was just wearing it so as to show off.

Anyway, when Narrow's boys came stumbling in, they was right at the top of their drunks, talking like none of them could hear and so as to make sure every one else did.

'Course being that juiced up, they wasn't too careful about who they was a talking about and sure enough they was blurting out something derogatory about one of the working girls. Something like, "Big Marge don't bed down no man whose feet don't smell least as bad as hers do!"

Well, right about when whichever one hollered this out, did it, out comes Greenbean Savage from Big Marge's upstairs sitting room, having just been sitting with her.

Now, if you were trying to find somebody in riding distance of Silverton that you wouldn't want to be crossing for no good reason, it would have been Greenbean.

It were bad enough that he'd been carrying around the last name of Savage when real savages was a burning and raping every thing West a

St. Louis. But on top of that, he had picked up the nick name of Greenbean from when he fell off his horse, sloppy drunk and smack into a just left plop of green, sick calf leavings.

Well, he was so liquored up at the time that he just lay there and slept through the night. The next morning, when he came ambling into town a bunch of the young'ns saw him with the whole side of his head all turned green and commenced to calling him "Greenbean". Well, it's a good thing they wasn't close enough to smell him, or they would have called him something worse.

Now folks never called him Greenbean to his face. But he knew they was using that handle for him behind his back.

Anyway, back to that night when he came out of Big Marge's sitting room to hear what he heard.

Now this would have been left alone if it wouldn't of been Greenbean what had just come out of Big Marge's room. But he'd been walking around looking for a fight to pick for some time now and he could tell that Narrow's boys was just drunk enough to argue back with him and so he commenced to being ornery with the boys and said he'd be back when they was sober enough to defend themselves.

Now here he was. Narrow and his boys sitting at one of the big card playing tables, and Greenbean standing just inside of the swinging doors with a couple of local prospectors.

This wasn't going to be no gunfight.

Greenbean was un-strapping his sidearm and commenced to saying, "Okay Narrow, it's either going to be you or which ever one of your boys wants to fess up to saying what it had been said!"

Now Narrow was the salt of the earth, the best lead wrangler as far as most folks could judge, and could ride down four good ponies in a single day. But he wasn't no fighter. Matter a fact, he wasn't built for fighting neither. You see, he picked up the handle of Narrow Gauge because he was skinny, like them tracks on the narrow gauge railroad they had spent the past year building to connect Durango and Silverton. This here was a special railroad being built narrower than most, so to fit between them narrow rocky canyons in order to avoid having to tunnel through them to the other side.

Anyway, Narrow had been brought in, as the first blacksmith foreman for the new line, clear from up in Great Basin where his Daddy had been one of them Mormon settlers what followed that Mormon preacher all the way from Missouri.

Narrow Gauge's Pa had been the first blacksmith in the Salt Lake valley, being known as the Great Basin since Jim Bridger had named it. Narrow's Pa had taught him the trade of blacksmithing. But Narrow had never hankered to the church learning they was insisting on and what made matters worse, was when his Pa came home one night and announced the Bishop told him to bring in another wife to help out around the place.

Well, this here new wife shows up and wouldn't you know it, this was the same girl Narrow had been seeing after dark up in the cottonwoods for prêt near two months.

So, next morning, Narrow walks into the blacksmithing shed and announces to his Pa that 'n angel had visited him in his sleep. And that he was leaving that very day, without purse nor script to do missionary preaching. Well, his Pa, being a miracle believing Mormon, saddled up his best riding horse for Narrow, gave him his best Sunday-go-to-meeting coat and top hat, and had his Ma pack him a two-day lunch. He then laid his hands on him blessed him that without purse ner script he'd be led to folks what ain't heard about the true religion yet, and then sent him on his way a blessing him out loud clean down through the town of Little Willow.

Well, Narrow headed strait for the supply wagon train he knew was heading for Silverton and got hisself hired on as the head blacksmith. With the exception of giving his Mormon Bible to one of them mule-skinners, he wasn't about to do no missionary preaching.

By the time they showed up in Silverton this boy had hisself the name of Narrow Gauge and everybody there had taken him in as a regular straight-up Cowboy.

Now, here he was staring Greenbean in the face and trying to decide if maybe he'd made a mistake, leaving that good Mormon upbringing where he could have been back blacksmithing with maybe half-dozen wives and a gross a kids running around the place waiting on him.

This here Greenbean was staring at him real mean like and there wasn't nobody breathing nor blinking,

This took some quick thinking on Narrow's part, but most everyone in that Saloon knew, if it was a thinking contest, then Narrow had the upper hand.

Narrow looked right into them squint eyes of Greenbean's and said, "They ain't no sense trying to figure out who it was had said what been said. Let's just settle her right here and since neither of us is carrying a side arm. I'm going to wrestle you and the loser takes his men and leaves."

Well, Greenbean breaks out laughing like he'd just been told the best story of all time and says, "Why you ain't got enough skin on them bones to wrestle my buggy whip. But if that's the way you want to settle this, I ain't got no complaint."

Right off people start to moving tables out of the way for what looked to be the shortest wrestling match of Rocky Mountain history.

Then Narrow says, "You know, there's a tribe of Eastern Injuns what wrestle to settle their differences because they can't afford to be killing each other off over squaws and such. If the way they do it's good enough for them, would it be good enough for you?"

Greenbean laughs again and snarls, "They ain't no way of wrestling where you could never beat me. So just say out the rules and get ready to lose!"

Well, Narrow makes old Greenbean lay down along side him, facing opposite ways and says, "Now all we got to do is at the count of three lift the legs that is next to each other, hook them and then you try to pull each other over to see who wins. Now have one of your men commence the counting."

Greenbean hollers up, "Jack, commence the counting."

Well, Jack does it kind of slow on account of he don't count so good and also so as to make sure Greenbean will be good and ready.

When he says, "three!" Narrow flings one of them long legs of his back, locks it around Greenbean's and before you knew it Greenbean has got both Narrow's boot and his own staring hisself right in the face, and he's yelling, "Let me up! Let me up! I wasn't ready!"

Well, everybody knows he was as ready as he was going to be because it was his own man that was doing the get-ready counting. But then, quicker than horse-fly wings flapping one time, Narrow is standing over Greenbean and says, "Since we might of said something to offend you and your girlie friend, I'm going to give you another chance."

Then he up and yells over to Billy the piano plays, "Bring me that broomstick from behind the bar. We is now going to do the fairest of all ways of deciding it."

He then got Greenbean to sit flat on the floor facing him with their boots sole to sole and heel-to-heel.

Then he says, "This here is called the stick pull. What you do is grab on to this here broom handle with your hands between mine."

They held the broom handle between them, knees bent, feet to feet and arms outstretched.

"Okay, now have you sidekick Jack there count up to three again, then all you've got to do is pull this broom handle and try to pull me over on top of you. If you let her go or get pulled over by me then you lose."

Greenbean says, "Jack, commence to counting and get ready to kick these boys out of here!"

Well, Jack takes his time counting again, but as soon as he says, "Three!" Narrow pops his legs out straight and jerks Greenbean clean over his head, crashing him right into Greenbean's own men, who was standing behind Narrow ready to pounce on him.

Another clean win by Narrow and the entire saloon commences to cheering while Greenbean and his boys limp on out yelling they been tricked. But knowing it was a fair fight and it wasn't never meant to be brung up again.

Least wise not by them.

CHAPTER 3

▼

TRADING FOR A BRAIDING

He'd been called by the name of Narrow Gauge ever since he worked on the Narrow Gauge railroad down there in Colorado connecting Durango with Silverton. But folks up here in his hometown of Little Willow didn't know about his Silverton history.

'Course he'd told everyone at home he was going off for missionary preaching and though that wasn't the fact, folks here at home still didn't know no better.

He'd heard his Ma was ailing from childbirth so he'd come on home to see her in case she was to die as a result. He ain't told nobody except for his old friend Port, who'd found out about his living in Durango and had sent word down with some trapper friends of his.

Narrow had come on up as fast as his best pony could make it without having to trade off for a rested one, and it had still took him two full weeks of riding.

This wasn't no small fete, given that he'd ran into heavy spring rains down in the red lands of Moab, and that red clay just stuck to his horse's hooves like the plaster Grandma Smith had conjured up for bad stinging-nettle burns and poison oak rashes.

This, coupled with the rapid rising of the desert streams over silt sand that sucked up a horses leg prêt near to a Cowboy's spurs, had slowed him up.

Sometimes all a Cowboy could do was find a rocky overhang and sit on a dry rock until things let up.

Well, Narrow made it through them storms and was sitting on the back porch of Port's trading post down near what Brother Brigham had named the Jordan River. 'Course it wasn't much of a river. Nothing like the Mississippi, the Missouri ner even the Red. But it did have some significance because it kind of resembled the real Jordan River that connected the Dead Sea and the Sea of Galilee according to the Holy Bible. Least wise that's what folks said inspired the naming of it.

Well, for Port, it was a good location since the wild weeping willow trees and the scraggly cottonwoods gave him the cover he needed for the secret coming and going required for hisself and some of his customers.

You see, Port had hisself a reputation that was good if you was telling folks about him, but not so good if you was him. To hear him tell it, it was just something he was supposed to do and there wasn't no other choice in the matter. He had up and saved the life of the angel-seeing Mormon prophet by the name of Joe Smith. Then, after Joe and his brothers had been shot down in cold blood the new Mormon leader Brother Brigham had kind of made Port his body guard in the event that anybody wanted to come on after him too.

Now Port wasn't a regular church going Mormon. But he knowed for sure that he hisself had been spared more than a few times for doing what the Prophet Joe had asked him to do. So he wasn't about to question what he was asked by Brother Brigham.

This here special assignment had given him opportunities to shoot down a few rascals what had Brother Brigham in their sights. As a result he had picked up the reputation of being some kind of gun-slinger.

Well, this gave Port a couple of groups of enemies. Those what was trying to get Brother Brigham and those what was friends of those who Port had killed while he was protecting Brother Brigham.

Story goes, that in order to compensate him for all the time he had to spend between Salt Lake City and St. George (Brother Brigham's winter home) protecting Brother Brigham, he had been set up with this Trading Post business in a prime location for trading. And in a prime location for sneaking in and out.

Nobody ever knew when Port was actually going to be in for trading, but that didn't matter much because he had one of the local boys name of One Arm Thompson to keep shop for him. One Arm had lost his arm in a wagon incident while helping to move granite stones for the building of Brother Brigham's Salt Lake City Temple when it first was begun about seven years back. Since he was doing a righteous deed when he lost his arm Port figured he deserved a steady means of making a living. Since Port hisself couldn't be around for no regular steady store tending, this was a good solution for them both.

Now One Arm was as honest as the day is long and more important than that, he was good at ciphering and pretty much kept track of everything for Port whether he was there or not.

Having a Trading Post in 'n area with a bunch of Mormons could get a little different than what you would expect. Your Mormons was supposed to do their trading with other Mormons and had to give whatever they didn't use over to the Bishop who figured out who needed what. Then he gave it out to them what was the most needy. So there wasn't much need for a regular Trading Post. But, truth be known, the outsiders, namely the trappers and traders and prospectors what come through on their way to hunt up gold in California or chase silver claims in Colorado was hard pressed to find anyone that would trade with them. The Mormons was funny that way. You pretty much had to join up with them or they was skeptical about doing business with you.

But, One Arm got on real good with these desperate traders and even though they was many times needy for supplies he treated them fair and didn't try to ask for their daughters as they thought he being a Mormon might do.

It was also said that if you wanted some tobacco or drinking liquor, this here trading post was about the only place you could get any between Cheyenne and nigh unto Sutter's Mill. Of course they didn't advertise this none. And when confronted by the local Bishop Port and One Arm would just say they had taken this here liquor in trade from a newly converted Mormon what had given up the evils of drink and tobacco and they was fixing to trade it off to the next pack of gentiles what came through.

Port had come to be good friends with Narrow Gauge for a totally different reason. You see, Port had been promised, by Brother Brigham, that like Samson of the Bible he would be spared if he didn't never cut his hair. He had held to this and had never cut his hair since.

Well, he hadn't give it much thought except for the fact that he dare not leave it hang down long from under his hat in case he was mistaken for a Injun dressed in white man's clothes.

One day when Port was fixing to leave, Narrow's Ma was down at the trading post bringing in some lye soap she had rendered up from pork rinds and such, looking to trade for some tobacco leaves to use on a lame mule.

She saw Port trying to get this huge mane of hair all poked up in his broad brimmed hat.

Ma says to him, "I ain't never seen such a grown man having such a way with hisself. What you need is a good braid'n job!"

Port looked at her (which wasn't too hard to do because folks from the entire valley knew she was right easy on the eyes) and says, "Well, if braiding can help me get my hair hid better, I guess you better be showing me what it takes to get this stuff braided."

Well, Ma says right off like he was one of her own young'ns, "You ain't never going to learn how to do it yourself. Take some of this here soap, go outside and stick your head in the horse trough and lather up that hair so as to take out that trail stench. Then rinse it off good and get yourself back in here."

Port knew right off that he wasn't going to leave until she was finished with him and commenced to ablidge her. He left his hat on the table and went out to do what needed doing.

When he came back, she sat him down on the cracker barrel and commenced to braiding them gun slinging, life-protecting locks like she was a driven woman.

The only other two witnesses to this was Narrow Gauge, who at the time was nothing but a seven-year-old whippersnapper and One Arm, who was afraid not to say nothing because he was afraid what he would say may seem sissified to Port. Even though Port was a friend, he still might pull that repeating pistol if he was irked too quick.

Ma just kept after all that hair, a pulling and a crossing this way and that for about fifteen minutes. Then she said, "Okay Mr. Body Guard of the prophets, see how quick you can put your hat on now!"

Port just kind of looked up at her like a puppy what had just been caught doing his business in doors and grabbed his hat and slapped it on his head.

You ain't never seen a man with such a mean reputation getting no wider a grin that what slashed across the face of old Port. That big felt hat went on slicker than it had been just measured for him. Fact is it went on and off so smooth that he just kept putting it on and taking it off about twenty times, just because it felt so good to do so.

The further amazing thing about it was there wasn't nary a long hair what fell down around his ears nor down the back of his neck neither.

Why he looked just like any other white man with a hat on!

Port turned to Ma and said, "Lady, you just made yourself into my personal hair braider. If you'll braid this up for me about once a month I'll trade you a different yard of gingham ever which time you do it."

Now Narrow wasn't old enough to see what just happened. But One Arm hadn't lost no brainpower when he lost that arm and he saw some kind of sparkle in Ma's eye that wasn't just because she had a hankering for some new gingham.

It didn't take her much thinking on it before she agreed to the arrangement, but only if it were kept a secret betwixt those witnesses what was in the trading post that day. Port agreed to let her know when he wanted the job done by tying a small strip of gingham on one of the branches of the big cottonwood up in the meadow. Once she saw it she was to excuse herself from whatever she was doing early the next morning and meet Port there to take care of the braiding.

Being a witness and all Narrow ended up going with her for most of these meetings. Part since Ma was afraid he'd let on what was happening and part because she wanted him to know there was just hair braiding and visiting going on.

No more and no less.

She being a married woman and Port being a single-man, wouldn't be right otherwise.

That was now many years past. Port still got his hair braided by Ma, but not near as often and it had been nigh on to ten years since Narrow had accompanied Ma down to the meadow. But over the years Port had kind of taken a liking to Narrow and had been the one what told him about that supply train going to Silverton what needed a smithy. Port had kind of just been as good a friend 'n older man could be to a boy growing into his own.

Now Narrow was sitting here on the back stoop of the trading post whittling at a root of scrub oak thinking back on that first day his Ma and Port had met. And trying to figure a way to see his Ma one last time without having to go through some kind of spiritual welcome home from every one in town what thought he'd been Bible thumping his way around the country side out East somewhere.

Port came out and sat down in the oak rocker aside Narrow and said, "You know, as sick as your Ma is, she ain't never one denied me a good braiding job. What say I send old One Arm over to visit in the buckboard just out of being friendly and have him slip her a slip of gingham. Figure she'll get out of bed to meet me?"

"I don't know." Said Narrow. "How bad she ailing?"

"Well, it ain't that she's real sick, its just that Doc Sorensen figures she's got some disease that she'll just die from and he figures she ain't got that long before it takes her."

Narrow kind of thought on what Narrow had just said for a minute or two. Then he said, "Well, it'd be prêt near like old times...and nobody seen us then. Is that meadow still as pretty as it use to be?"

Port looks at him and answers, "Yup, and them first alfalfa blossoms are opening up with this moisture we been having. Not to mention some real nice tasting watercress that your Ma's been harvesting down there. You know she even planted some of that rhubarb so she'd have a good excuse to excuse herself when I needed her."

Narrow nodded, "Let's give her a try. If she's too sick to make it then I'll expose myself to whatever spiritual welcome-home the town has to dish out. If not, I'd like to see her with you there, just like it used to be."

One Arm got things arranged and the next morning as the Howlett's roosters was a crowing, and the magpies was a calling for a bright blue day there came Ma, just as pretty as she'd always been, carrying her basket for watercress and rhubarb with a couple of extra combs in her long braided hair.

She saw Port first because Narrow was kind of concealing hisself behind the Cottonwood they usually sat under. Since it were that she didn't know this, she up and gives Port a big hug and a kiss smack on the mouth like they was a couple of courting teenagers out where nobody would see them.

Narrrow came out after that embrace and Ma no sooner saw him than she got tears in her eyes like she was crying happy. And she was.

She gave Narrow a bear hug. He looked up and there was that smile on Port's face just like he remembered it some twenty odd years ago. Then he knew for sure that it wasn't just for no good braiding job neither.

CHAPTER 4

▼

DYING FOR YOUR BELIEFS

Folks say that them kids back East in them clean clothes and fancy hats had been reading about how exciting the West was, and that there wasn't nothing but brave men and stalwart women out there a taming the untamed.

Well, any Cowboy worth his salt would tell you, that what them Easterners had been a reading wasn't no more based on fact than a buffalo can fly. Why half the grown men that died out here died out of plumb fright when their tickers just gave up from the worrying about all the ways they figured they was about to die!

Take B.A. Washburn. His Daddy had come on out here with most of the other settlers what had been following the Mormon leader by the name a B. Young.

B.A.'s Daddy's name was Seth Washburn and he'd been studying some pretty heavy book learning at one of them fancy Eastern schools when he got convinced that young Joe Smith had seen angels telling him to start a new religion.

Seth joined up with the believers back when they was first getting started in up-state Pennsylvania and had stuck with them clean through them being run out of Ohio, across Indiana and eventually Illinois and Missouri.

In the process of getting run out of these places he'd picked up a couple of wives, a mess of kids (half of whom had died from all the hardship) and worse of all he'd picked up a down right obsession for learning about Injuns.

Most folks figure it was that advanced book learning what made him so dang curious. But the truth of the matter was that he was scared nearly religious over the possibility of being killed by Injuns. Somehow he got that feeling all turned around to acting like he was interested in every thing he could collect about them.

Due to this book learning ability, he made a living for hisself and his wives and kids by teaching school. Taking stuff in trade for teaching basic reading and ciphering and doing this most of the time from the back gate of a Conestoga wagon, or just pulling the youngsters together after suppertime. But there wasn't no single student what didn't come away from him without finding about what kind of arrow heads the Apaches used, or what kind of huts the Navajos lived in, or how the Sioux used every part of the buffalo to some use or another.

Seth finally settled down in Little Willow, which was located prêt near twenty miles South of what Brother Brigham had named Salt Lake City.

Brother Brigham had figured out how to set up boundaries on as much land as was livable and some that wasn't. He sent folks for settling new towns everywhere he could, East of the Rockies, South to the Mexican border and West to what folks was beginning to call California. To accomplish this he'd send out several wagon-loads of families to different points, tell them to build a fort for protection from the Injuns and then to get some crops in before Spring was run out.

Little Willow wasn't no different in so far as it were settled, except for they was hunting for a school teacher and had been real grateful when Seth shows up with his wagon-load of family members and second wagon-load of Injun relics.

Truth be known, they would of welcomed anyone claimed to know book learning, being it was true or not. When you got yourself thirty or forty families living within the confines of some kind of closed in fort, things could get a might too neighborly for even your neighborly folks. You add to this the fact that most of these families consisted of no less than three or four wives and fifteen or twenty kids…well now you got yourself a major baby sitting problem!

Fact of the matter was, school learning wasn't nearly as important as getting them kids out of the way of folks that was trying to scratch themselves a living before the Injuns came, the crickets ate their crops or they found some way of getting water to their kitchen gardens.

Now, the first night Seth and his bunch showed up a town meeting was called to rightfully introduce and welcome them.

Once the introduction was finished by old Bishop Browning (who was eventually to take credit for bringing book learning to Little Willow) Seth hisself stood up and said he was going to throw in some learning for the parents what might prove to save their lives one day.

He then commenced to spinning out yarns about the Injuns he'd learned about. For you knew it his wives and kids were walking between the rows of folks, showing off things of what he was referring to. There was your tomahawks, your throwing knives, your special throwing hawks, arrow heads of all shapes and sizes and these made from all sorts of metals.

He then had hisself beadwork and braiding goods the likes of which most whites had never laid eyes on, at least not these folks what was getting more scared by the minute.

Now Seth wasn't no all-time showman. But given that the closest these folks came to being entertained was when old One Arm Thompson would let folks watch him try to tie his own shoe laces with one hand, or ride a horse with reins in his mouth while shooting a long rifle, Seth could tell when folks was getting down-right interested. And he was not for disappointing them neither.

He kind of paused for a minute, causing a hush to come over the crowd, and then he says, "Folks, I been praying for some time that me and the wives would be led to a special place to settle and commence to raise up our young. When I was first asked to come out to Little Willow I told the wives I had to do some thinking and praying on it and so I saddled up one of the wagon horses and took a ride out here all by my self.

What I found was something that I know you folks ain't aware of. Of course if you was, there would probably be most of you wouldn't of stayed on. Being knowledgeable as I is in what I found, I figured I owed it to you good folks to take this here teaching assignment so as I could be here to help you with what I expect is a problem, you just ain't aware of."

Seth stops speaking for a moment or two and just looks out at folks like he was looking special at each one. He then turns to Bishop Browning and says, "Is these here folks faithful and committed to settling in this here little valley? Because if they ain't, I ain't a going to be the one that lets them know what they is in for, and then having them leaving a place what they been proper assigned to by the Prophet Brigham hisself!"

Bishop Browning (not wanting to speak for no one what ain't been given the choice hisself or herself), stands up and says to everyone, "Everyone what is faithful and committed to settle in this here little valley called Little Willow no matter what Mr. Seth Washburn has to say, raise up your right hand and be counted".

Now, Mormon folks always had a tradition of raising up their right hands for prêt near anything when they was asked to do so from the pulpit and so did these here folks on this night.

"Any apposed", Bishop Browning asked.

And now, no one raised their hands on account of most Mormons didn't believe in being apposed to anything what it was they was asked to do by their church leaders.

That being taken care of, Seth turns back to the entire group of towns-folk and says, "Folks, while I was picking my way on horseback out through the scrub oak and tumbleweed, not three miles West of where I is standing at this very moment, I come across some serious Injun artifacts."

He stopped at this point and kind of let folks suck in their breaths and turn to each other whispering what he had just said.

"Now these here artifacts ain't the kind of artifacts what I been letting you look on tonight. Folks, these artifacts what I discovered is nothing less than a sacred Ute Injun Burial Ground."

No sooner had he said what he just said, than Sister Lovina Fitzgerald fainted dead away, right into the arms of Brother Sherman Kimball who was standing behind her.

Well, it didn't take more than a couple of minutes to revive her and then Seth went on, "Now folks, if there's any more of you that's got weak knees or prone to fainting, what I got left to tell you, you better not stay to hear."

He stopped and stood for a minute while the women got a little closer than their husbands, and some of the young had their ears covered by their protecting Mothers.

"You see," he said, "this here sacred Injun burial ground has been used for many generations of Injuns. And like graveyards of white folks, Injuns mark their graves special ways with special writing that I've learned me some ability to cipher. But folks, it ain't them old graves what has me worried…it's the evidence of new graves what I need to tell you about."

As a direct result of that last comment, down goes Sister Fitzgerald again, and folks finally decided she ain't got no constitution fit for this here Injun education. So a few of the men carry her on over to a wagon and without reviving her they just laid her in the wagon and came on back.

Seth continued, "Now, from what I can cipher there's been dead and buried in this Ute Sacred Burial Ground as recent as last fall."

This brings on another hushing and whispering.

He goes on, "And folks, what has me especially worried is that them Ute's is known for going South for the winter, following the buffalo and then coming back North for the summer for hunting in the cool Rockies, picking up fresh supplies of salt for preserving red meat, and most of all, paying respect for their dead at their Sacred Burial Grounds."

Well, this here news brung up a few shouts from the townsfolk.

"It's prêt near summer already!"

"What if they don't like us this close to their dead!"

"This here fort ain't nearly big enough nor good enough if a whole tribe of Ute's attacks us!"

Seth puts up his hands and says, "Folks, I didn't mean to upset you, nor your wives nor your young'ns. I'm afraid I did though and for that I apologize. Fortunately, I been studying on Injuns enough to where I got a solution to your problem. I'm going to need me twenty strong men and a couple of teams of horses to leave with me right now for that Sacred Ute Injun Burial Ground. If this ain't possible, we may have ourselves a problem to contend with in less than twenty days when I figure them Ute's will be coming back."

Bishop Browning got a raising of hands for the men that had no excuse not to volunteer and these men commenced to kissing their wives like as to never see them again and decided that riding the teams was easier than walking that three miles to who knows what might commence to happening.

Seth led out on his saddled-up team horse and then had one of his wives drive the wagon what he used for keeping his Injun artifacts right behind. He also instructed the men to approach the graveyard quiet like and respectful so as to not interrupt the spirits that were dead.

Well, these angel-believing men stayed in right close and made sure to keep a count on the number of torches they was carrying from the town fire.

About this time, the proprietor of the only Trading Post for non-Mormons by the name of Port was a coming South from Salt Lake City where he had been a protecting Brother Brigham from a suspected group of undesirables that had wandered in from Missouri. Now, Port ain't never cut his hair on account of being told that if he did he would surely die. Since it was nightfall, he wasn't wearing no hat so his hair was a flapping in the breeze. To make matters worse, he was riding bareback on a big paint mare what was part of a trapper trade he was culminating that very night.

No sooner did he ride over the sandy ridge of the North end of the valley, than Seth looked up hollering "INJUN!" in a voice like as to scare a scalp off a white man and then he up and fell clean off that team horse he was riding.

Everybody else knew it was just old Port. Heck, they would recognize him anywhere. So they just ran over to Seth, and Doc Sorensen, being one of the volunteers, asks one of the boys to shine a torch down. There was Seth, his eyes clean open, his mouth still in the act of yelling "Injun" and his hands clenched to his chest…deader than one of them recent dead Injuns.

There he lay, his ticker not a ticking no more. Killed by his own fright of seeing 'n Injun.

Well, folks set out the next morning to look for that Ute Sacred Burial Ground. After two days of looking, they gave up on finding such a place. But out a respect, they decided that the proper place to bury Seth was on 'n unusual hill they found prêt near exactly three miles West of the fort.

Now one of the duties what old Port was to carry out for being allowed to run his Trading Post, was supervising the digging of proper graves. So he hired on a passing trapper what needed to trade a day's work for a grubstake and had him commence to digging. Well, this old trader wasn't no more than two feet down when he commenced to clanging his shovel into all kinds of Injun artifacts. Now Port, being used to secret keeping (due to his special calling of protecting Brother Brigham) decided it was best for all if he just kept his mouth shut and went ahead and buried Seth right down there with what he died for believing in.

Story goes, some many years later, folks indeed discovered that hill for being a Sacred Ute Injun Burial Ground. But by then the tombstone of Seth's had disappeared and his remains was dug up with the rest and put on display at some museum and labeled as being some of the best preserved Injun bones what ever been found.

Well, that's the story of how S. Washburn had died. And truth be known, it wasn't that unusual from how most Cowboys died a taming the old west.

CHAPTER 5

▼

OFFICIAL U.S.
GOVERNMENT SECRET

The East and West railroad was about to be connected near the South-east corner of the Great Salt Lake. Narrow had signed on with the rail-road, as a blacksmith like he had been for the Narrow Gauge line down in Silverton. He had decided to stay in the Great Basin valley after coming to visit his friend Port and his ailing Ma.

Turned out, his Ma had some kind of miracle healing from laying on of hands from one of the more spiritual Mormons name of F. Parry. This F. Parry had married a daughter of One Arm Thompson's by the name of Joy.

They had met out in California where she had been sent to help with some relations. These relations had been right there with the Sutters at Sutter's mill and prospected out more gold than they knew what to do with. So they had sent for Joy to be some kind of permanent live-in baby sitter and maid.

No sooner did she get there than this feller Frank Parry had come in off a Merchant Marine ship and seen her doing the family marketing at the General Store. He got one good look at her and commenced to asking folks who she was, but found out that he wouldn't have no chance of being properly introduced unless he was to get hisself baptized a Mormon.

F. Parry didn't no more know what a Mormon was than a coyote knew how to give birth to no Billy goat. But that didn't bother him none because he had spent the past two years aboard ship and visited places where squinty eyed folds had believed all kind of strange things.

So he commenced to finding out who was in charge of Mormon baptizing. Turns out, his name was Bishop Adamson. At least wise that's what Frank had figured his name was because that's what folks had told him. He ain't never met nobody with the first name of Bishop. But that didn't intimidate him none. He figured he better put his best foot forward. So he put on his dress Navies and headed over to where he'd been told this Bishop Adamson lived.

It was a hot August day, and before he knew it he had his jacket off and decided to roll up his sleeves. This is something he kind of liked doing anyway because he had some of the biggest, strongest forearms in the Navy. Usually just walking in somewhere with them arms hanging out was as powerful as if he were wearing a couple of six shooters.

Frank also had hisself a couple of real nice tattoos, one on each arm and each with a special memory.

Well, that walk over wasn't getting no cooler and Frank, not being used to the dry heat what he was experiencing started to get him a case of heat stroke and just as he got to the Bishop Adamson's front stoop, he keeled right over. Most folks would of figured he was nothing but a drunken sailor, but even though that weren't the case he was passed out anyway.

Well, Frank slept right there all night.

Next morning, Bishop Adamson opens the door and prêt near kills hisself, tripping over what appeared to be a drunken tattooed sailor sprawled all over his stoop.

The tripping over him wakes Frank up just enough for him to say, "I come to be baptized a Mormon."

Bishop Adamson looks Frank right in them bloodshot eyes of his and says, "Sailor, we is having a baptizing right this morning. Sinners is welcome so come on with me and we'll take care of you before you sin no more."

Frank was baptized, not ever remembering what happened the night before. But Joy Thompson was at that baptizing ceremony to witness her niece's baptizing. She saw Frank and like folks say who witnessed it, "it was love at first sight".

They was married less than two weeks later and came on back to Little Willow to settle down.

To make a long story short, Frank had discovered that them big arms and hands of his was better for healing the sick than wrestling with sailors. Of course it wasn't for him not still doing some wrestling. Every chance he got he would volunteer to wrestle anybody for the amusement of townsfolk at special events and town celebrations.

Since Frank had healed Narrow's Ma, Narrow decided to stay on at Port's for a while to make sure the healing took good. In the process of waiting on his Ma staying healed, this historic event of hooking up rail lines from East to West right here in what they was calling Promontory Point was about to happen.

Narrow figured that it might be right nice being a part of this history. Matter of fact, word was that some of them reporters and tintype photographers from back East newspapers was heading in for the final hammering of the final spike.

But right now, Narrow had something else on his mind. It wasn't no more than half a day's ride to the cold spring stash up in what they was calling Little Cottonwood Canyon. And he made that ride a couple times a week to pick up stored vittles for Port's Trading Post. For most Cowboys that wasn't nearly enough to get up a good lather. But for Narrow this was aright painful experience.

Reason was, a couple of days back, the boys on the rail crew had come up short handed and Narrow volunteered to give up his smithing work to help swing a rail spike maul. He knew the work wasn't easy. But figured it couldn't be much harder than anvil hammering which he'd been doing from dawn 'til dusk at his Pa's Black Smith shed.

About the third swing of that maul and his back had went out like it'd been stuck with about four Injun arrows all at the same time. Now this had happened once before, right after he'd tried jumping down from one level of switchback track to the other level back in Durango. That jumping had give him broke down arches in both feet which didn't hurt his back none, but while recuperating by laying in bed with his feet strung up to the ceiling rafter one of the working gals from Big Marge's over in Silverton had came over to provide some bedside manner. Well, while she was in the process of administering that bedside manner is when his back give out the first time.

He kind of remembered that experience now.

Funny how pain under good circumstances can kind of be lived with and not forgot.

Since he couldn't swing that spike maul, no more, and beating on a smithing anvil wasn't possible neither, he'd been assigned to make the daily ride up to the cold spring stash with a pack pony to bring down supplies. This was better than not working, but the long ride really pained his back something awful.

With every step of his riding pony, he got to thinking about how it pained his back. If he only had something to rest his back on, it may just help a little.

He remembered that when at home his most comfortable sitting position was sitting on a oak rocker with his feet up on the porch railing. This was even easier on the back than laying in a feather bed on a straw stuffed mattress.

Narrow could fix prêt near anything that got broke or needed to be working better. And he just kept thinking on this. For you knew it he was back to the company smithing shed sketching out what he expected to call the Narrow-back saddle. Named after hisself of course.

He'd already thought about hammering the back of a wooden rocker on the back end of his saddle. But figured it'd be pretty hard to get wood hammered together well enough not to fall apart under the stress of horse and rider.

So he was figuring on smithing a saddle with a high back out of wagon wheel rim steel in one piece being smithed from the horn at the front of the saddle to a high backed seat at the rear. The thing would be covered with smooth leather with the grommets and stirrups from a ordinary saddle fixed proper to their place.

Between fighting his back pain and making his daily runs to the cold spring it took Narrow prêt near two months to get his basic design hammered into metal. He also wanted to avoid interlopers seeing what he was working on, so most of what he did, he had to do when the regular smithy was out fixing a broke wagon or at the rail site inspecting the special trusses and other fabrications what needed inspecting.

In the meantime Narrow'd already had his friend Port working on the leather cover and even incorporated a suggestion of Port's that later on proved to change the entire purpose of the Narrow-back saddle.

While Narrow was so busy working on this special project, he plumb lost interest in what was happening out at Promontory and truth be known, he didn't plan to ride out no more for the big event. Matter of fact, that very day was the day he and Port had decided would be the trial ride date of the Narrow-back.

Just as a matter of principle, Narrow and Port worked through the entire night before putting the leather cover on, sewing on the stirrups and riveting the cinches.

By dawn of the day they was to drive in the golden spike at Promontory, Narrow and Port was ready to saddle up one of Port's best riding horses with the strangest looking contraption what ever been placed a top a Cowboy's best friend.

There she was, crafted just like she'd been made at one of them Kentucky saddle making shops. And rightly so. Narrow was as skilled as he was clever.

"Well Narrow," Port said, "I think we got ourselves something special here. Climb on up there and see how she feels."

Now Narrow already had been rehearsing this moment in his mind for over a month and he didn't have to be asked twice. Fact of the matter was that the basic design had been modified just thinking about how to mount up. Ordinarily a Cowboy would put his left foot in the stirrup of a regular saddle then swing his right leg on over. But the original design Narrow had would of kept even a long legged Cowboy from getting his leg high enough to clear that tall Narrow-back. So Narrow had cut the back clean off of his original design and then reconnected her with a couple of heavy bolted door hinges. This allowed for the saddleback to be laid back down straight for mounting and dismounting and then pulled back to the upright position and locked in place for your long-term riding. Not only that, but the bolting in points was covered with extra heavy padded leather that fit the small of your back like it'd just been made for it.

Like most of Narrow's inventions it was the cleverness built into it, what made for it being a might more useful than most folks would appreciate.

Now all this explaining aside, Narrow mounted up, snapped that Narrow-back up against his still ailing back, and got hisself a smile on his face like he'd just won the greased pig chasing contest over at the Little Willow Pioneer Day's festivities.

Port even took off his hat…like not knowing it, he was paying some kind of respect for something almost religious in nature.

"Narrow", Port Said, "I want you to ride that saddle down past the big bend in the river, then come on back and tell me how she feels."

Narrow was pleased with the feel. Of course it wasn't his nature to be totally satisfied, and he was thinking about some changes he'd make on the next one. But this was about the most easy on the back, pony ride he'd ever took.

As Narrow finished that first test ride and came back within sight of Port, he saw hisself a stranger standing next to Port. At first glance Narrow figured this stranger to be some kind of U.S. Cavalry. But as he got closer he could tell it was a uniform he ain't never laid eyes on before.

Soon as Narrow brings his mount up close, Port says, "Narrow, I'd like to introduce you to United States Special Agent Boberg. He's here on special assignment from the President of the United States hisself."

Narrow respectfully snaps back the Narrow-back so as he could swing his leg over, dismounts and says, "Glad to make your acquaintance."

"Son," says this here Special Agent Boberg, "I'm here on special assignment of the President to witness the connection of the two railroads. But your friend Port here got word to me about this new saddle of yours a couple of weeks ago when I was down here picking up some drinking whiskey for myself and others what needed it. After thinking on it for a few days I got back to Port and asked him to have you screw that wooden back on to the backside of it without sharing the reason for wanting it."

Narrow nodded and replied, "Yes Sir, I is still not right sure what purpose it has. But Port insisted for reasons he said he'd share later. Knowing he's a man of many important secrets I just did as he asked me, and did so without pressing for no reason."

Special Agent Boberg answers, "From what I can see, this here saddle may have a special and important purpose for the United States Government. You see, most folks know and appreciate the special need for the Pony Express. But we've taken that one step further. That being using special long riders for carrying confidential papers of the President and other United States government officials to points of the West that ain't got no telegraph wires nor mail service. We been looking for a saddle design for these long riders that will give them some relief for back aches just out of being naturally tired. But more important, what really impressed me was the protection the rider could get of being back-shot from bullets and arrows by having a high back on the saddle.

We have learned that most renegade Injuns would back-shoot our messengers, then just let them ride off with arrows sticking out of their dead backs. They figured that maybe the horse would lead them back to the closest fort or Cavalry bivouac. This gave us the idea that if our long riders knew they was entering Injun territory they'd just carry a couple of arrows in their saddlebag and stick them into the back of that Narrow-back saddle. This being done, they would give Injuns the impression they had already been back-shot. This allowing them to ride on through without any real harm coming to them.

'Course, in the event 'n Injun or outlaw did try to back-shoot one of these riders both the wood on the back and the metal wagon rim on the inside would stop prêt near any arrow or bullet for that matter."

Port then stepped up and says, "Narrow, Special Agent Boberg here has been authorized to pay you top dollar for this here saddle. And also pay a mighty handsome price for the private use of your design, which is to be kept secret and used for only special government purposes."

Well, by now, Narrow was dismounted and listened to this entire conversation, not hardly believing what was being said. Of course, he didn't need to think on it. He just looked at Special Agent Boberg and turned to Port and says, "Port, I'm just a Cowboy and a blacksmith. So I'm relying on your judgment. If you think this is a fair price, then I ain't got no reason not to want to do right by the United States Government."

That being said, Port turned to Special Agent Boberg and said, "Tell your boys to bring that wagon around."

Special Agent Boberg let out a whistle, and around from the stand of cottonwoods down by the spring, came a single-horse-pulled U.S. Government issued short wagon with two drivers and a covered short bed. He then turned to Narrow and while handing over a leather pouch said, "Your government is grateful and proud. But remember, this here's a highly confidential transaction, and Port here being our witness, we ask for your word of honor that you'll never reveal nothing about the Narrow-back, nor never tell no one who it is that is using it, or what for."

Narrow took the pouch and without even looking inside answered, "Yes sir Mr. Special Agent, I is honored to keep this secret."

Well, they was gone as quick as they could get that Narrow-back loaded under cover of that wagon.

After they left, Port and Narrow just kind of sat down on the first step of Port's Trading Post watching the dust left from behind one official U.S. Government Special Agent on horseback, and one official U.S. Government issue short wagon.

After the last swirl of dust had settled, Port turned to Narrow and asked, "want to go on up to Promontory Point and see history in the making?"

Narrow just kind of turned that leather pouch over in his hand a couple of times and replied, "No, I figure I've made my own history. I expect I'd like to just sit up on your rocker, with my boots resting on your porch railing and relax my back until the sun sets for the day."

Well, neither Port nor Narrow never heard about, nor never seen the Narrow-back saddle again. And far as they knowed, it became one of the best kept official U.S. Government secrets what ever been kept.

CHAPTER 6

▼

SCRATCHING OUT A LIVING

Your ordinary Cowboys pretty much knew how to do some basic doctoring, both for themselves and on their stock. And Narrow wasn't no different.

But this here skin rash he'd caught hisself was just down right impossible to doctor.

Seems he'd been taking his weekly bath down at the North end of the big lake, and when he waded on out he'd brushed up against some kind of extra powerful stinging nettle. Least wise that's what he thought he'd done.

Now ordinarily this kind of problem was just lived with and went away slow, but wasn't no cause to interrupt no Cowboy's regular work. But it'd been nigh unto two weeks now and Narrow still only got relief if he had hisself chin deep in cold water, or was sound asleep. That is if he could get hisself to not scratch long enough to get no relief.

To make matters worse, Narrrow had just signed hisself on as the lead wrangler for a cattle drive leaving from the Great Basin within a matter of days. They was going North to a newly staked-out high-mountain ranch up near a Northern Lake what they was calling Bear Lake.

This wasn't to be much of a cattle drive given those what Narrow had been on before. But this Bear Lake ranch was little further than half way to them hot spring pots and geysers what Jim Bridger hisself had discovered and called the Yellowstone area. Narrow was right curious about seeing that part of the North Rockies and signed on as a kind of excuse to head that way.

But as things was right now, there wasn't no way this Cowboy was going to be able to sit still guiding a herd with this here constant itching and resulting scratching.

Fact is that Narrow's scratching from this plague of red bumps and blotches had got on to his friend Port's nerves so much, that Port had made Narrow move his sleeping mattress out on the stoop at night.

Folks just don't appreciate how uncomfortable things could get for Cowboys when things couldn't get any more uncomfortable.

Narrow had even accompanied Port over to visit Ma for the regular monthly hair braiding and she'd tried applying some of her special plaster ointment. His hopes was high that this was going to help. But after Ma's doctoring the itching wasn't any less nor the resulting scratching letting up neither.

Tomorrow was the day set for meeting the herd down West of Utah Lake and Narrow was sitting in the porch rocker out front of Port's Trading Post thinking on what he was going to do, when in comes riding a feller by the name of G. Mouritsen what most folks referred to as Glen.

He was riding his favorite mount, a big black and white paint with his yapping dog riding right behind him on his horse's rump. This on account of the fact that he had trained that little dog to jump up on prêt near anything, moving or not, and stay there as if his life depended on it until he was told he could move. Why he even had him so as he would jump up on milk cows, mules, and billygoats and even little spots like the top of a fence post or a moving wagon tongue just to show off how good that dog was. If he was told to, this yapping little pup would jump way up on the seat of one of them big wheeled bicycles whilst the rider was standing up peddling around town. And there that dog would sit, just as sweet as you please, round around town 'til he was told to jump on down.

Anyway, Narrow had known Glen for some time, but was a little surprised at seeing him out here at Port's.

Narrow had still kind of been hiding out from towns folk on account of he still hoped they was thinking he ain't back from what they still expected was his being back East missionary preaching.

If he wasn't so miserable scratching hisself he might of got out of sight from Glen. But he was plum sick and tired of being sick and tired and figured maybe Glen would provide some interesting conversation that would take his mind off all what was ailing him, and possibly give some useful advice.

Now Glen here, had hisself a quite unusual profession that prêt near qualified him as being as close to a animal doctor as a party could find West of the Great Divide.

You see, Glen was called in to help your bulls and your stallions with their mating problems. Of course this wasn't something you would talk about when there was women folk around. But it was a service what needed doing and Glen had figured out some right clever ways to get her done.

There ain't no need a getting in to the details here about how he did what he did. But working with 'n excited bull or a jumpity stallion with a bunch of in-season cows or mares was a job to be respected.

Anyway, all this expertise around important livestock kind of got him a reputation of some kind a animal doc. So folks sent for him if a foal wouldn't stand up, or a cow got bloated, or a milker started to get hoof rot, or if a de-horning or castrating didn't stop bleeding.

So as Narrow sees Glen riding up, he figures he might just ask him about this here rash.

As Glen dismounts and steps on up to the door of Port's Trading Post Narrow says, "Hey there Glen, is you on some horse breeding mission or can you sit and visit for a while?"

Now Glen really wasn't one to have to be invited for no visiting. Matter of fact, truth be known, one of his great secrets of getting them stallions and bulls to get on with their breeding activities was just visiting with the rancher or farmer until eventually the deed was done. Of course the real secret was that them livestock just didn't like folks watching their romancing, so soon as Glen got folks in to a nice yarn and they quit watching for the mating to happen, it usually did.

What Glen had to say was usually quite interesting and most folks came away feeling pretty good about wasting a couple hours. But then most hard working folks was looking for a reasonable excuse to take some time away from the plow or the hoe anyways.

Now when it came to visiting, the all time champion of the valley was a feller by the name of N. Bateman. And rightly so.

You see, even though he was a feed peddler by profession, his real calling had been politics which had eventually made him one of the first elected mayors of the Great Basin. This happened because he knew everybody from visiting with them when he was making his grain peddling calls. Everybody bought feed from him, but it wasn't from him being what you would call a masterful peddler. It's just that after visiting with Noal, a farmer or rancher kind of felt that buying grain from him was the least you could do after everything you'd been told.

Why a body could start at day break just meeting him, (referred to by most folks as Noal) at the irrigating ditch by accident and before you'd knew it the sun would be setting in the West and he'd have you all up to date on every living soul what ever been born or died since before your granddaddy's granddaddy. And he'd even commence to speculating on folks what ain't never even been born yet!

His ability to do this was down right amazing, and his reputation was such that if a party were late getting anywhere and somebody asked why it is you were late, all you had to do was say, "Well, I'd of been here prêt near on time, but I ran into Noal on the way over."

Now you might think this would sound kind of disrespectful of him. But folks just liked him so much that if they heard that excuse for you being late, they wouldn't be upset about you being late, they would just be upset that they wasn't lucky enough of being with you when you had your visit with him.

Then they would commence to asking you to try and remember what all had been said and see if you could repeat the high points…knowing full well that nobody, saved for Noal hisself, could remember all them names and relations.

For Cowboys like Narrow, visiting with folks that knew a whole lot of other folks was prêt near the best entertainment that could be hoped for. Real Cowboys were a might bashful and didn't speak up unless they was spoke to. Least wise that's how Narrow was on most occasions. And listening and nodding to a good yarn was about the best relaxing a Cowboy could ask for.

But back to Glen riding up to the Trading Post.

Narrow figured, what with his animal doctoring knowledge, Glen here might know about curing of stinging nettle rashes. So Narrow figured he'd up and ask him what about some advice.

Narrow barely says, "Howdy do," and Glen, being always looking for new information, first asks Narrow about how the missionary preaching went and why it was that nobody knew he got back yet neither.

No sooner did Narrow tell Glen about his smithing and wrangling down in Durango and Silverton and finished swearing Glen to his Mormon Bible honor not to tell nobody, than Glen starts to spinning a tale about the last time he was on the Eastern side of the Rockies.

Now even though Narrow had been out of town, so to speak, for some time, he remembered hearing this here yarn from Glen once before. Not that it mattered none, because a tale worth hearing once was usually worth hearing again, especially if you kind of let on that it might be the second time you heard it. Then you would kind of get a new version that more times than not had some more interesting information. Glen and Noal was both masterful at this re-telling of stories better than before.

Well, just about this time in the visit, in comes Port riding from the North like as his life was endangered.

Port hisself wasn't generally one for stringing more than a couple of words at a time together and almost never interrupted a visit from Glen or Noal. But as soon as he lit down off his pony he didn't excuse hisself ner nothing. He just says, "We got ourselves some major trouble coming in through the Emigration Pass. I just reported to Brigham Young hisself that there's 'n official U.S. Army heading this way to take control, even if it means the spilling of blood on account of folks back East figure we are out here starting our own country."

Glen speaks up right quick and says, "What does Brother Brigham expect we ought to do about it?"

"Well," says Port, "Right off he sent me and one of his Apostles up to see if we couldn't slow them down. So we snuck in at night and untied their saddle horses and then scattered them before daybreak. That being done we figured they would be slowed down for prêt near a day or two just trying to catch their horses. But right about day break one of them Cavalry buglers blows his 'time-to-wake-up-the-troops-for-inspection' bugle call and danged if them dad-burned horses didn't all come running back to camp like they was meant to be inspected themselves!"

Port goes on, "Brother Brigham is now inspired that rather than get ourselves in a war with what we still believe is our own country, he would send out some of the better educated men all dressed in their

Sunday-go-to-meeting clothes to sit down and see if they could have some kind of pow-wow before any blood gets spilt."

"But boys," says Port, "While they is hoping for a peaceful resolution, they've come up with a plan to hide out all the towns-folk within the next three days. They want it so as that if that army rides in to town, they'll find themselves nothing but loose laying hens and wagon tracks. It figures that if there ain't no people to take control over, there ain't no reason to stay."

This being said, for once and the only time in his entire life, old Glen seemed to be at a loss for words. He just kind of swallowed hard and looked over at his dog. That yapping dog of his had even shut up and looked like he was prêt near ready to get down off that porch post on which he was perched the entire time of all this visiting. Funny how critters kind of know what it is what's going on.

Narrow swallowed hard hisself and says, "Port, when I rode in a few months back I came in through the upper Alpine pass South East of Little Willow. There's plenty of water up there and a good stand of high grass for grazing."

Port replied that he knew the area well and getting wagons up there would be no problem for the townsfolk.

Glen agreed to get hisself over to Mayor Bateman's so as to get the word out proper. He also promised not to do no visiting with Noal once he got there, because both he and Noal would have to see everybody in Little Willow by sundown with the news to leave.

Port had to get hisself around to about twenty more settlements in the next two days, and Narrow had to get hisself over to the ranch were he had to get that cattle drive leaving early if they was to avoid being caught in any army shooting. Or worse, have that U. S. Army confiscate them high priced breeding stock for slaughtering purposes.

Before he left though, Narrow asked Glen for some advice on this here rash of his.

Glen looked at him real close and says, "How long you been wearing that shirt?"

Narrow says, "Ma just sewed up this here wool shirt up for me on account of how happy she was I came on home for a spell. But we don't have time for no visiting about no shirts. What I need is help getting rid of this here rash!"

Glen says, "Well, that is what I mean. You got yourself what doctors call a allergic reaction. You see, some folks just can't wear no wool because if they do they get themselves a rash that ain't going to leave until they quit wearing what ever it is wool they is wearing.

Why I even heard about a Cowboy what was allergic to his own hat! He thought he had hisself some kind of head lice. So to make matters worse he kept his hat on at night so as to not let any more lice in.

Well, that not working, eventually he even shaved his head, his beard and took some sheep shears and cut the mane and tail from off his horse. He figured if there wasn't no hair for them lice to live in, they would just fly away.

Didn't you know, this here last idea did eventually solve the problem. Seems that the day he shaved his head, he decided to take hisself a dip in the local stream and tried to keep his head sunk under for as long as he could hold his breath for to get some relief. In the process he got hisself a head sunburn that made his scalp redder than if he'd had 'n expert Injun scalping.

He didn't notice this sunburn until he slapped on his hat that the next morning and wearing that hat hurt like he'd never had no hurt before. So, not being able to wear his hat, he dipped his kerchief in the creek and tied it over his head like a granny going out to church. Well, while he was waiting for that sunburn to heal, he lost his hat in a dust storm and within two days his rash was gone. He didn't know what it was that had healed him until he rode in to town on Saturday night and was bragging up to the local gals how it was he got rid of his head lice and was looking for some companionship. And he was also telling folks about his sunburn and losing his hat.

The town barber was sitting at the card playing table with the rest of the boys and also being the town dentist he knowed right off about allergic reactions and commenced to explaining the whole thing to this here red headed Cowboy."

By the time he had finished this yarn Glen had helped Narrow off with his suspenders and that wool shirt. Narrow wasn't right sure if he was to believe this here story about the hat. But neither hisself nor Glen had time to speculate on the eventual outcome, what with people to warn and cattle to drive.

Glen rode off at a fast gallop with his yapping dog sitting on that paint pony right behind him and Narrow finished gearing up his pack pony for what he was hoping would be a lot less scratching and a lot more Cowboy'n in the days to come.

CHAPTER 7

▼

COWBOYS ARE THINKERS

Horses are like human beings, except for they are better than human beings because they don't never change much.

You see, if you got yourself 'n ornery horse, that horse will probably be ornery day in and day out and for his whole life.

Human Beings, on the other hand, may be ornery in the morning and then be nice as you please by sunset. Or, glad to see you one day and then ready to shoot you down the next.

Figuring out a horse is a task you only got to do but one time. But figuring out a human being…now that could take you a lifetime of trying.

That is with the major exception of Cowboys. Cowboys are human beings as close to being horseflesh as a creature could be, without having hooves or eating hay.

Like horses, Cowboys are either mean or hard working or neighborly or ornery or a whole lot of other things. But whatever they is, they don't change much ever so long as they remains a Cowboy.

The interesting thing about this is that there's many a ornery horse that's got hisself a real neighborly Cowboy and visa versa.

This ain't through any outright planning by your average Cowboy. It's just that Cowboys generally picked their horses out of limited choices. And it took a good deal of luck to get yourself a mount that had itself the same kind of temperament as what you has or what you want it to have.

The right frustrating thing about it is that a Cowboy usually would out live the usefulness of a good horse about every two or three years. Not that the horse died off that quick. Heck, given a good home, horses was knowed to live prêt near forty some years. On the other hand, a well-treated Cowboy was darned lucky to see his fortieth birthday. It's just that so many unfortunate things could happen to your mount.

It may seem unlikely, but prêt near every Cowboy, by accident, shoots down one of his own horses at one time or another. One way of this being done, is by trying to shoot a sidearm from saddleback while at a full run and pulling your trigger right when your pony decides to jump a prairie dog hole. Your own dang stupidity is then immediately rewarded by finding yourself flying across the prairie at full horse speed, while your pony's laying dead some thirty feet back, with your own gun's bullet hole right between his ears.

Cowboys have also been known to shoot their own ride home by leaving them tied up to a tree when out hunting in the fall quakies for deer or elk or moose. Then proceeding to getting themselves walking around lost, only to eventually come up on the back side of their horse right at twilight. And thinking it was a deer, or a elk, or a moose, back-side-shooting their own perfectly good horseflesh.

But besides shooting your horse by accident, generally your broke legs and normal trail diseases is what took down most ponies. Then a few is rode down by desperate Cowboys who was doing it to save their own skins from Injuns or outlaws.

Anyway, when a Cowboy needs a new mount, for whatever reason of not having his anymore, generally he wasn't somewhere that there was a big choice of good horseflesh. If there was, they usually wasn't for sale at a price a Cowboy could afford.

If he was lucky enough to be near a livery, there was usually fifteen or twenty head to choose from. But a few was usually just green broke and couldn't yet be trusted. A few more was too swayed-back to where mounting up meant dragging your spurs in the trail dust. And then there'd be one or two would have hoof rot or dry hack. Then if a Cowboy was lucky there would be one or two left what wasn't in heat or had been gilded too old that could be choosed from.

So picking yourself a pony that had your kind of temperament, kind of came last on the shopping list. Especially for a Cowboy that had to get back on the trail before his herd turned around and headed back to where he was bringing them from.

Narrow had been lucky in this regard. Or at least he had planned to be lucky.

He had found hisself a real pretty black mare down in Durango that came from good breeding stock. She was prêt near seventeen hands and had been broke by a rancher that ran a large string of ponies in with his breeding cattle. So she was use to working stock from dawn until dusk and didn't spook from 'n antsy bull or overly protective cow that had just calved.

But like every horse, she had herself a temperament that was just her own.

First off, she had what most Cowboys would call the "wild eye". Meaning she couldn't be forced to do what didn't come natural. Now cutting stock and roping for branding and long term riding and drinking when she was led to water is things what came natural. Least wise they did to her. But tying her by the head, either with her reins or by a normal hitching rope didn't come natural to this mare. Why when being tied, she had been knowed to break every thing she'd been tied with, or just pull so hard she'd end up sitting down like a long eared mule, and then waiting until some sorry Cowboy could get that rope or rein knot untied to let her go.

Once Narrow had figured this out, he just never tied her no more. This wasn't that much of a problem because she'd stand still where ever he left her just by dropping her reins. She might graze herself a few feet here and there. But it wasn't like she was going to head back for the barn or get spooked by a jackrabbit, or even take off looking for greener grass.

For a Cowboy that only left his horseback to allow for night grazing, this here problem could be lived with and Narrow had just adapted hisself to it.

But there was one other thing that this here mare didn't see as natural, and that was having a tight saddle cinch.

Most Cowboys knowed that your smart ridding pony always bloated themselves out when you was a cinching them up, and then let their breath out just when you got your boot set in the stirrup and was about to swing yourself on up. This usually left your greenhorn and his saddle hanging from the belly of 'n animal what knew it just outsmarted a human being.

This wasn't exactly the problem with this here black mare. She'd let Narrow get the blanket and saddle all fixed on her back, and even commence to looping in the leather straps of the cinch. But soon as that cinch touched her belly she'd just go plumb loco until you loosened her up again.

After a couple of months of pulling the cinch tight only to have this mare rare back and roll over on the saddle like a hound dog trying to give hisself a back rub, Narrrow had just plumb decided to give up. Matter of fact, there was many a day when he just rode her bareback and left the saddle back home just to avoid the whole situation.

It was on one of these bareback riding days that he ran hisself into the feller what sold him this stubborn piece of horse-flesh.

This fellows name was N. Vawdrey.

Now Vawdrey was about the best judge of horseflesh in all of Durango, and owing to the fact he also broke this here pony hisself, he was down right set back when he saw a working Cowboy like Narrow riding her bareback.

Now it is important here to mention that by this time, and owing to these here problems, Narrrow had give this horse the name of Kant. Like in you "can't" tie her and you "can't" tighten up her saddle cinch.

Now naming your horse was one of the few privileges what a Cowboy had. Usually a smart Cowboy took hisself a few weeks before he conjured up a proper name for it. This so he didn't find hisself calling his mount by some name that just wouldn't make no sense by what kind of horse habits that new horse had. Then finding hisself ridiculed by the rest of the punchers for the entire length of the drive. Not that ridiculing each other wasn't going to happen anyway. But getting your horse's name all involved just didn't serve no smart purpose. That is if you could help it.

Vawdrey up and asks Narrow what he's doing riding around with out no saddle.

"Why even the Injuns is fashioning themselves saddles these days!" says Vawdrey.

Narrow, being somewhat embarrassed, pushed his hat back and said, "I don't mean to be disrespectful of your selling me this here working horse. But she's been giving me trouble with saddling her, and I just about plumb give up with trying."

Vawdrey dismounts and like he was serious about making things right with his friend Narrow, he commences to taking off his own saddle and says, "I was out mending fences the day you came in and picked up this horse and I'll bet you my foreman who handed her over to you didn't explain to you about this mare and her saddle problem."

Vawdrey says, "When we first broke her, we was using a new saddle and unbeknownst to us, this here saddle had a cinch that hadn't been properly finished off. It had some rough edges on it that just cut right into this mare's stomach like she'd been leather whipped. We didn't figure this out for prêt near two weeks trying to get her broke. By the time we finally did, she was cut up pretty bad and we just had to turn her out to pasture for a month of healing. When she was finally ready she was so shy of being saddled that we couldn't even come close with a saddle without putting blinders on her. This eventually helped us get her saddle broke. But by the time you came to get her, she still wasn't what you would call enthusiastic about being saddled. But we learned that if you put some lambs wool on your cinch, before hand and then slapped her on the neck just before you yanked that cinch she'd already have her flinching over and then you had best mount her quick. The combination of lambs wool, slapping and cinching and quick mounting kind of solved the problem."

Vawdrey then shows Narrow what he means with his own saddle and then commences to apologize for not having his foremen give these important instructions at the outset.

Narrow was thinking back on that day back in Durango this afternoon as he was heading down to the East side of the big lake to get this breeding herd ready to move on up to the North end of the Great Basin. Kant was moving along at a nice smooth trot and the pack pony was kind of loping along at the end of Narrows leading rope to keep up. Not to give the wrong impression, Kant had some right redeeming characteristics including a trot that was so smooth a Cowboy would almost be able to take a nap while clipping along through the scrub oak trails and tumbleweed plants. This was a darn sight easier on Narrow's back than most riding had been, and for that he was a might grateful.

The August sun had dried up most of what lived between the mountains and there wasn't no wind except for what these two ponies left in their wake. It was the beginning of another Cowboy trek and except for the allergic rash Narrow was expecting to be almost over with, he was feeling good about hisself and getting back on the job of cow pushing.

Long about mid-afternoon, Narrow stopped to give hisself and his ponies a drink. It had been prêt near three months since he'd been away from civilization on what you might call a permanent basis. And as he laid down upstream from his stock and stuck his face in the cool mountain stream for his drink, he started to feel that lonely anticipating that he and most Cowboys got as they was just ready to head back out to the trail. The feeling was good and gave him some comfort of knowing this was where he belonged.

Like most Cowboys what used up their young lives out sucking in dust from behind the wrong end of cattle herds, Narrow felt right comfortable by hisself or with only one or two human beings near by. You rode your horse and did your job and only had worries that God and nature placed before you each day.

Sure, a Cowboy would think on what it might be like to have his own ranch, or prospect up a stream full of gold. But ever thing he really needed was shared between him and his two ponies.

A Cowboy knowed hardship was just around every corner. But living through the heat of a North Texas cattle drive in August, or suffering the misery of a two-day cloud burst slopping through red clay, or freezing your handlebar mustache clean to your face on the cold of a desert night, or even experiencing a stampede while you are sleeping and finding yourself woke up nearly dead and left with nothing to your name but your long handled sleeping britches…yup, these was just a part of Cowboy'n. And for the most part could be lived with.

Heck, Kant here can't be tied nor cinched easy. But these wasn't no big worries. Narrow's last horse bit every human being what came near him. The one before that was so scared of people he had to be tied and left outside of town with the hope he wouldn't be stole by Injuns or outlaws.

The actual thing of it is, that a Cowboy is one of God's few creatures what spends most of his life just sitting and thinking. Your good horse learns to do all the cattle driving work by the end of the first week. So most of the time a Cowboy's just sitting up there to make sure the saddle horn don't get caught on some low hanging branch.

Narrow, having got his drink and had some chew a deer jerky, mounted back up and headed on into the shadows of the Western mountains and commenced to speculating on just how much horses could think. And whether they really was as much like Cowboys as he was thinking they was.

CHAPTER 8

▼

SQEETERS AND SINNERS

The Magpies was screeching down at their morning prey. Meadow-larks was singing out their everyday tune what since folks came West, every prairie mother had added her own words to. And the Killdeer was skittering out in front of the herd so as not to be trampled.

It had been prêt near seven days since Narrow had got hisself a suitable bunch of cowpokes together and started to move a herd of breeding stock from the West end of the big lake to the valleys of the northern Rockies.

It was a strange time of year to be moving a herd North. But a Cowboy's duty was to move cattle and not question as to why or sometimes even who for they was a doing it.

On the first day out they had seen from clean across the valley, settlers from his home town of Little Willow moving themselves and their families and stock and wagons, up through Corner Canyon to where they hoped would be a temporary safety in the high mountain alpine meadows. It appeared that Port's warning of oncoming U. S. Government soldiers had made it through and folks was taking it serious. Narrow knew or was related to most every soul on that trek. But from here all a Cowboy's eyes could make out was the slender outline of a string of wagons and the late summer dust they was kicking up.

Narrow's horse took off after a stray calf and by the time Narrow looked back from hanging on to this bit of Cowboy'n, all sight of that small-town wagon train had disappeared into the shadows of the mountains.

In spite of all their independent and hard-headed ways, Cowboys was a sentimental bunch and Narrow wasn't no different.

He had hisself things to do now and them memories of the past summer was being downright overwhelmed by the job at hand.

Seems this herd a breeding stock wasn't eventually headed for no dinner plate back East. To the contrary, this here mess a hoofs and horns was planned to be the prime breeding stock for a whole new part of the Rocky Mountain West. They wasn't longhorns neither. They was solid black, carried themselves low to the ground and had themselves a way of carrying more than their share a beef. They also didn't move as fast as your longhorns nor other range cattle and this is what had Narrow worried. Like most foreman, part of Narrow's foreman agreement was to give some kind of guarantee as to when the job would get done.

Even though they was well past the pure salt that'd been washing up from the Great Salt Lake, this here drive was already two days behind after only seven days of moving. Now, Narrrow had to decide whether to chance a steep trail through a pass that hadn't never been used to drive cattle before.

This decision wasn't no worry over the stock making the up-hill grade. The real fretting was if there might be 'n early winter storm and whether they might get froze in beneath deep snow.

Narrow had sent a puncher out a couple of days ahead and he'd returned with a notion that three or four days might be saved by taking this here pass.

He'd seen some sign of trappers. But no sign of Injuns ner settlers that would complain if a herd were to come through and tramp down the creek beds. He also said there had been some frost every morning. But no sign of snow yet, though there was still some summer glaciers left on the shaded end of the high pass lakes. The quakies was just starting to turn and there was plenty of grazing grass. He also reported that there wasn't no rivers ner streams that would have to be swum across.

This here particular puncher was a good friend of Narrow's by the name a Howdy Gaigen. There ain't no such real name as Howdy. But then no Cowboy would never be letting hisself be called Howard neither.

Howdy made hisself out to be such a good scout due to his down right obsession for fishing. Folks that don't understand fishing most likely don't savvy how a fisherman makes hisself into such a good scout, or Cowboy for that matter. Truth be known, Howdy had devised hisself a means of fishing what he had picked up in part from some Mexicans. This on account of living across the border for a spell with his polygamous kinfolk. They moved down there on account of they was scared of what may happen to them if they stayed up in the U.S. Territory, what with all their wives and such.

Howdy was showed by these Mexicans that your worm fishing wasn't possible South of the border. This on account of there wasn't no plentiful supply of worms down there. Seems it was just too danged hot and sandy for your usual fishing worms and night crawlers to survive. But instead of worms, what these Mexicans had was mosquitoes the size of baby humming birds. They would thread them whilst still alive, right on the hook, then cast them out to float and buzz right on top of the creek what they was fishing in.

Well quicker than a frog could take a fly, them Mexican fish would swallow that hooked skeeter and you'd have yourself your dinner a hinging by the end of your fishing line.

When Howdy growed up and moved back up North, he couldn't find hisself none of those big south of the border skeeters. So he started experimenting on using all kinds of other bugs. What he found was that your northern cold-water fish hankered for bugs what was the smaller the better. But this created a problem for Howdy because he couldn't get no hook through one of these little critters without them just falling apart in his fingers. So he come up with the idea of conjuring up his own creations of what looked just like bugs, but was made out of horse hair or cottonwood seeds or milkweed parts or cattails or you name it. If he could make it look like the right kind of bug, he'd use it. This kept both man and beast a might jumpity when Howdy was around because if he saw a hair just the right color a growing out from the back of your neck or the top of your ear, he'd just pluck her now and thank you later.

The real artful part of this was in the knowing as to what kind of bugs your fish were biting on. This was where old Howdy learned his scouting abilities.

Why, he could tell what was going on in a place he'd never been before just by what kind of bugs was buzzing around. While your Cowboys was swatting away these no account varmints and your ponies and herd was flitting them with their tails and hooves, old Howdy would be trying to catch hisself one so he could tell you if it had been a dry spring or a heavy snowfall last winter, or exactly what kind of fish there was going to be for dinner that night.

This Howdy was right smart enough to be a Cowboy and for that Narrow was grateful. In particular since the rest of this here gaggle of ain't-going-nowhere Cowboys wasn't exactly the best what had ever tried moving a herd nowhere.

But back to this mighty important decision what had to be rendered about taking this high mountain pass. Narrow trusted Howdy's judgment and decided to get the herd headed up this new direction for settling in for the night.

Now getting a herd of cattle to move in any given direction was about as easy as pushing a snake up a tree from it's tail end.

But just knowing this made the job somewhat tolerable. Your new cowpunchers what ain't never had to do this before was your frustrated ones. Unbeknownst to Narrow, he had hisself more of these new ones than he'd suspected when he'd signed them on.

See, what with your church approved ability to take yourself more than one wife at a time, most of your ordinary Cowboys had figured staying home and hitching up two or more hard working wives to tend to your needs was heaven sent better than eating cow dust for a living. What this left for Narrow to choose from was nothing but drifters and boys what had to leave town for reasons of their own.

With the exception of Howdy, these boys had been born and growed up, but the brain part of their up bringing had got inherited by somebody else.

Do to this bad Cowboy'n situation, Narrow was making hisself dizzy riding around then entire herd as fast as he could and as many times as he dared not to count before nightfall.

It wasn't right that 'n experienced Cowboy and the lead wrangler at that, had to work so danged hard. But Narrow wasn't one for slacking and just kept his kerchief up and things moving while trying to make these Cowboys act prêt near half as smart as the cows they been hired on to move somewhere.

By the time the early fall stars finally broke through the blackened sky Narrow was leaning against the grub wagon and having hisself a nice morsel of cold stream trout what Howdy had brung in. He and Howdy was the only ones was still awake and Howdy had agreed to take half the night watch so Narrow could get some well deserved shut eye.

The trout was good and went down right nice with some larded up pan-fried potatoes. Narrow was tired, but he knew it was tired that was coming, so it wasn't no surprise.

He no sooner got his boots off and hisself laid down than he gets woke up before he's even asleep by the worst Cowboy singing he'd ever heard. Matter of fact he didn't even figure out it was singing until he decided that there wasn't no way a squealing pig and a mad laying hen could be here on a cattle drive and trying to out noise each other.

Once he had hisself awake enough he realized it was old Ned who must a brung hisself a bottle of Doc Sorenson's drinking liquor, and was singing off the results. Now Ned and Doc Sorenson was the only regular drinkers could be found in Little Willow. Narrow had brung on Ned to this cattle drive only out a hoping he'd get him sobered up. And also out a feeling some obligation, beings that Ned was his first cousin and they both kind of came from the same stock.

Ned and Doc Sorenson both have pretty interesting stories. But as Narrow was thinking on them and this bad liquor singing, he just fell into a Cowboy sleep and ended a day that had been a lot longer than a Cowboy could stay awake for.

CHAPTER 9

▼

EAGLE'S NEST

The fresh morning snow squeaked beneath the Cowboy's leather boots. Bawling cattle could be heard from up and down the canyon walls. The first storm of the early fall had been kind to Narrow and his bunch, leaving only a couple of inches with longer leaves of grass still piercing upward, hoping for the melting sun.

The drive was on the downward side of the pass and the lost days had been picked up thanks to Howdy's good scouting, and a bit of luck from Mother Nature. Not that all the fretting was over, but the fretting that could be planned for was, and for this Narrow was a might grateful.

This here skiff of snow kept the trail dust down and for once in a few times your pushers from the rear wasn't needing to wear their kerchiefs over their faces. To make the drive even a might easier these here short black cows had proved to be right smart and kept themselves head to tail behind the lead stock.

Stock are a lot like human beings. After moving around together for a while they kind of have their leaders and their followers. And things get to be somewhat organized.

Narrow should of knowed that this here easy going wasn't meant to last. But renegade Injuns wasn't in his immediate plans neither. These here was a bunch of Blackfoot that had been drove by stand up Injuns and uniformed whites to these high mountain passes. They was on the look out for whatever it would take for survival and had themselves painted in solid body paint, half face black and half face white. They was prêt near invisible coming through the winter quakies with ponies that was either black and white paint or butt speckled greys.

Narrow knowed right off that if they didn't want to be seen they wouldn't have been by now. Nope, they wasn't trying to sneak in for no attack. They was just intent on coming in face to face with a small bunch of cowpunchers pushing critters like they'd never seen on four hooves before.

Narrow hadn't had much experience with Injuns. But about two days back a trapper name of E. Giles had come up on Narrow and asked if there was any need for additional help.

Well, Narrow knows that the only difference between your Cowboys and your high mountain trappers is how you spend your time when there ain't no cows to punch. So he asks this here Giles feller if he's willing to stay for the duration. Giles agrees to these terms and that being agreed to he falls in right to being as good a wrangler as Howdy, and even takes on extra night shifts while Howdy's out scouting.

Seems that Giles was prêt near as clever as Narrow. When he wasn't trapping, Giles had been working with your milking farmers inventing all kind of new ways to get the milking done.

Now sending your daughter or wife out with a three-legged stool and a wooden bucket to tug on old Bessie was good enough for your family milking. But when it came to collecting milk in any kind of quantity for hauling to market, you either had to have yourself a slew of daughters, a bevy of wives, or some kind of other solution.

It was these other kind of solutions what Giles' had become knowed for. Seems he'd convinced some of your bigger farmers to get themselves steam engines all hooked up to all kinds of pipes and contraptions to where they could milk themselves half dozen head of milkers at one time, without no help from daughters nor wives neither.

Seems that one of these big dairymen what Giles had done all this inventing for had his spread in 'n area what was occupied by friendly Injuns. Giles had learned to speak some Injun, and more important, make your Injun arm and hand signs.

Since Narrow figured these here Injuns wasn't here to do no killing or it would of already been done, he hollered for Giles to come over and be with him when the Injuns got close enough to pow-wow.

Giles knew right off what these Injuns was up to. He pulled his mount up along side of Narrow and said, "Keep your eyes on them Injuns and don't look over at me neither now ner when they get up close. We want them to figure we is both wise to them and I'm going to make you that way in the next minute or two we got until they get here."

Giles proceeded to then tell Narrow about the spiritual nature of Injuns being their weakness. He figured that he'd just let them come on in for a closer look-see.

Well, once the head renegade got within about a hundred yards, he then sent a brave in on horseback right up to within spitting distance.

Giles whispered through his bushy red mustache to Narrow, "Keep your head up and look him right in the eyes. Don't blink ner act scared. I'll do the talking. You do the intimidating."

Now contrary to your normal Injun what is slow to speak and then only grunts out a few words, this here brave was down right excited and must of blabbered out every Injun word what ever been grunted before Giles could even ask what for!

Then, just as quick as he started, he just shut up, turned his mount around and then headed back, joining his feller braves and they all turned and left a whooping war cries like they had just killed off the entire United States Cavalry.

Narrow and Giles just watched those Injuns ride their ponies off down through the valley and out of sight until the only sign of them having been there was the faint echo of Injun calls, bouncing off the granite rock cliffs and cold lake glaciers.

Giles turned to Narrow and says, "You're going to have to increase my pay."

"Why's that?" asks Narrow.

"We just been told we've got ourselves a herd of sacred buffalo calves." Says Giles. "And to make matters worse, them Injuns are going to make sure we don't make these cows do nothing they don't want to do."

Narrow swallows his fear and asks, "What'd they mean by that?"

"Well," says Giles, "They figures we is Injuns dressed like whites being sent here by the Great White Buffalo to watch the dead spirits of honorable dead Injuns what been rewarded as being sent back as sacred black buffalo calves. As caretakers we is also to be worshiped. That is until we do anything what them Injuns thinks ain't sacred to them sacred cows we been driving."

Giles, not ordinarily being much of a talker neither, then takes hisself a long swig of water from his deer stomach drinking bladder and then goes on. "Narrow, we best get this craggily bunch of buckaroos in here for some Injun educating."

Narrow whistled to Howdy and told him to get the boys in for some serious planning.

This Cowboy round up only took about half 'n hour.

When they was all dismounted Narrow commences to introduce them to their new problem when he notices Ned ain't among them.

Narrow asks, "Where's old Ned?"

Howdy looks up from picking stones from his horse's front hoof and says, "Couldn't find him and figured he must of come on back by hisself."

Well the boys all looked at each other real quiet like, and even their horses quit their fly swatting and snorting.

They all knew, and most of them had seen the Injuns. Narrow figured they was all thinking the same thing. When in the silence of thinking about what might be, down through the quakies comes Ned's mount, with Ned sprawled over the horn, his arms flapping down both sides of his mount's neck.

Funny how horses are so danged stubborn sometimes. But when it comes to their Cowboy being killed they always manage to bring him home.

Ned had hisself two ceremonial Injun arrows (being identified as such by Giles) shot clean through his back with the copper gilded heads poking out through his heart.

Giles pointed at Ned's right hand and said, "There's your reason for him being brought down."

Ned's right hand was still clutching to a long willow he had been using to prod some stubborn calf.

"Fellers," say Giles, "Them Injuns will be with us clean up to Wyoming. You will never see them and they won't even bother us if we just keep ourselves from doing nothing to hurt nor aggravate these cows. Ned here wasn't so lucky and didn't even know he was about to meet his maker for doing what comes natural to most Cowboys."

There was some respectful quiet while Howdy and Narrow pulls Ned down off his mount, pulls out them ceremonial arrows, and hands them over to Giles.

Narrow tells the boys to mount up and circle the herd back into the meadow. They would stay for the day to give Ned a respectful burying.

Giles told Narrow that they best give Ned 'n Injun burying to confirm them renegade Injun beliefs that they was sacred Injuns passing for whites.

So while Narrow, Howdy and Giles commenced to build a high burying platform, they reminisced on Ned's life.

He'd been the first dairyman in the Great Basin. Had hisself the largest herd of Holsteins what had ever been milked West of the Missouri. But he had got hisself involved in drinking Port's trading whiskey. His wife had taken over the running of the herd, but eventually the hard work had took her down and she died still a young woman made old from doing a man's job.

Ned tried to step in and take over, but betwixt the grieving of his wife dieing and the evils of drink he lost the whole kit and caboodle. He spent his last days, before signing up for this drive, just begging off neighborly relations.

He was a good man what just had hisself the wrong bad habit.

By sundown the burying place was ready and it took most of the boys working together to lift Ned's body up to the top of the burying litter.

Injun legend says that if your bones are picked by the eagles, your spirit will live on to soar above the earth forever. In a way, Narrow kind of felt good for Ned, meeting his maker this way. It kind of made up for some of the poor hands he'd been dealt the last years of his life. He also knew that when word got back to kin back in Little Willow, he'd be remembered as a brave Cowboy what died a honorable death.

That night was quiet and being the Cowboys knew them Injuns was keeping watch, all of them including Narrow, Howdy and Giles took a Cowboy's night off and fell asleep watching the early winter stars making a silhouette of Ned's peaceful body.

CHAPTER 10

▼

PROMISES OF PARTNERS

Narrow got that herd into that new high mountain ranch within two days of what had been promised. He collected hisself his regular pay and on top of that a bonus for having to bury one of his men on the trail. He split the bonus equal with the other punchers and they all split up for to seek out their next Cowboy'n jobs.

That is except for Narrow, Giles and Howdy who had decided to move on north to them geysers and hot springs they'd been curious about.

Winter was just settling in, but long as they kept themselves long what was called the Snake River the snowfall didn't slow them down much.

Narrow's horse Kant led out keeping the rest of the mounts in a steady canter. For the most part, these three Cowboys just kept one eye on the scenery and one eye out for Injuns or other trouble.

Howdy kept the frying pan full of fresh trout, salmon and pike, while Giles would mix in all kinds of roots and herbs he collected along the way. The eating was good, the nights was warm under buffalo blankets and the winter was still yet friendly.

Long about a week up river, Narrow and the boys comes up on a feller what introduces hisself as J. Butler. Says he's got hisself a winter cabin about half day's ride up river and being right neighborly invites them to follow him on up for a couple days of chewing fat and showing them around the strange places to be seen.

Just about nightfall they come around a bend in the river to see a sight they'd hear about but never figured to be laying eyes on. Right out there about a hundred yards ahead was a spout of steaming water, shooting clean up as far as you could see. And round about it was all kinds of bubbling pots of water and mud and what looks like lard a coming to render.

These Cowboys just sat there with their mouths hanging open. Then this here Jay feller hollers out, "Come on boys, it's bathing time!"

He then dismounts and commences to strip off his outwear, riding britches, boots and even his long-handled underwear and starts heading, butt-naked, for one of them big mud pots. Then danged if he didn't throw hisself right in...a hooting like a Banshee, smack in that mud butt first, laying out there like he was ready to float hisself silly.

Narrow, Giles and Howdy just kind of look at each other shrugs their shoulders and follows him in like a bunch of schoolboys out playing hooky and skinny dipping on their first serious day of spring.

Your ordinary Cowboy ain't much for bathing anyway, but bathing in mud what is black as the insides of your pony's ears was something new to all three of these buckaroos.

This here mud felt like the softest down what ever been plucked from a baby goose and oozed twixt toes and other parts like as to make you never want to get out.

Well it didn't take these kids in growed up bodies long to get downright silly looking at each other covered in coal-black mud. Before you knowed it just the sight of them had scared Kant and the other horses clean back into the pines where they just kind of peered out twixt the snow covered boughs waiting for what next from these crazy human beings.

By now they was on a first-name basis with this Butler feller and he says, "Okay boys, get your slippery butts out of here and follow me."

He then commenced to run about thirty yards, stark naked except for a entire coating of black mud, to another hole in the ground and then jumps into the air and falls down clean out of sight.

Having gone this far, this pack of why-not-he-done-it-first Cowboys head out like a flock of drunken magpies and jump into what appears to be a huge pot of green pea soup. Turns out it was just about as hot! Fact of the matter is, if these boys hadn't jumped in all at one together and being covered head to toe by mud, they may never of done it. But once they was in, it was too hot to move toward getting out and so they just kind of stood there, up to their necks in green bubbling water while the mud slowly washed away.

Meanwhile this here Butler feller was a laughing until he was crying.

"Cowboys," he says, "You just been officially greeted to the best wintering place in the entire West. Now that all that mud's gone and as a lasting memory, come on out. I've got something else to show you."

Once these Cowboys was out, standing on a nice warm rock, Jay commences to laughing again and says, "Now friends before I get myself dressed, take a good look at me and tell me what you thinks is different from 'n ordinary human being."

Now howdy, being the best tracker, notices right off and says, "Jay, you ain't got a hair on your body below your chin. What's wrong with you? You sick or something?"

Then Jay says right back, Nope, I just been body scalped and so have you."

Sure enough, Narrow, Giles and Howdy looks down at themselves and sees they is as hairless as a new born baby.

"Yep," says Jay, "The combination of that good oozing mud and this here green hot spring will pick you clean every time! I do her at least once in the fall and once in the spring to get rid of what ever critters I picked up from sleeping in my old buffalo blanket the rest of the year. But no need to worry yourselves none, it will all be growed back by Christmas and except for a little itching here and there, it's a might good for you. This here is just one of the miracles of these parts. It also works for plucking sage hens and skinning squirrels."

This not being lost on Howdy, he says, "You know, I bet this here would be way to scale your extra scaly warm water fish!"

"Scale them!" says Jay, "I use this here hot bubbling pot over yonder to cook them. You just catch them from the river, leave them right there dangling on your hook and dip them in this here bubbling pot for about as long as it'd take you to get your plate ready. Then you got yourself about the best poached-fish dinner what no rich city banker never ate, in no fancy, wear-your-best-britches eating establishment.

By now Howdy's got his clothes on and is tying hisself one of them home-made fishing mosquito hooks to the end of his fishing line. Howdy's one Cowboy what don't have to be asked twice to bait up!

Turns out this Jay was a down right good feller. After a early supper of fresh-caught bubble-geyser-poached salmon, he up and says, "Boys, that's just your first course. Take a gander at what I got here."

Out of his vittles pouch he pulls the biggest dad burned potato these boys had ever laid eyes on. Fact is, they first thought it was some kind of gourd or brown squash or something.

"Now boys," says Jay, "Take a look at what we been growing about two week's ride West of here. This here tater was grown from your ordinary tater seed. But we found ourselves a entire valley of rich, sandy soil what, due to the entire absence of any rocks, lets your ordinary taters grow as big as they get until the winter frost is just about to freeze them black. That's when we dig them up and make a Sunday family dinner out of just one of them.

Jay then jabs his throwing knife into this huge tater, ties his rope on the handle and dangles it into that same boiling hot pot what they poached that fish in.

"Any you boys got any bacon fat?" he asks, "After I boil the skin off this tater we'll slice off portions the size of flap jacks and give them each a quick fry in that fish pan."

Narrow says, "I got the lard and it'll be ready quicker than a school-marm's ruler hits a cursing boys knuckles."

When it comes to vittles, Cowboys ain't never got the right to be particular about what's put before them. Most times it is just pinto beans been soaked for a day then mixed into bacon fat or lard drippings. If you are lucky, and a might clever, you might also have yourself a start of sour dough what you can fashion yourself a biscuit or two from. But being that they wasn't particular didn't mean they had lost all their taste buds neither. Matter of fact they was probably more appreciating of a good meal than most any other critter what ever sat down to eat.

Truth be known, over good meals is where most lasting partners is found.

These four Cowboys was just putting together a friendship what miles, hardship and old age ailing wasn't never going to change.

They spent that entire winter teaching each other trades they had each been expert at. Narrow taught the best of blacksmithing. Howdy spent winter nights showing how to tie fishing bait to look like natural flies, gnats and other buzzing critters. Giles worked with all the boys in getting a wooden pipe contraption configured to feed hot water from one of them hot springs right in doors so as to have hot bathing and washing water right in the cabin. And Jay just kept everybody entertained by showing ways to scratch yourself when them prickly short body hairs start to grow back in places what couldn't be reached for scratching naturally.

It was a Cowboy winter to be remembered.

When they finally broke camp in the spring they all promised to meet back next winter, come hell or high water.

Howdy headed Northwest to where he'd heard there was fish as big as human beings what would swim up rivers right from the sea.

Jay was heading back to seed his tater farm, and hoping to name these taters the Butler spud.

Narrow and Giles both headed back south for the Great Basin. Narrow still had the sorry duty to take back the sad news of Ned's being killed and return his personal belongings to his kin.

Giles heard that Brigham Young hisself had commanded the faithful to start church operated farms and it just figures that they would be needing some fancy milking contraptions.

Well, a Cowboy's promise, like these partners had made each other to meet again, was always meant sincere, and for that it was trusted. But it also came with the unspoken understanding that if it wasn't kept, it wasn't because it wasn't meant to be.

CHAPTER 11

▼

GOD'S PAY

If you ain't never seen the high mountain deserts in the spring, then your years as Cowboy has been wasted. The smell of wet sage and the beauty of sego lilies and cactus flower is one of the few things what brings a working Cowboy to stop and take in what it is that God Hisself created.

Coming back from up North, Narrow had stopped by at Port's Trading Post just long enough to have Port ask him if he'd join him for a special trip he had to take down to St. George. The weekly train from back East had brung in some new strains of pecan tree seedlings and Port had been asked to get 'n open Conestoga wagon load down to what they was calling the Mormon Dixie for some late spring planting.

Narrow had agreed and besides, Giles who had rode down from Yellowstone with him had taken on a job with a feller by the name of Kay Smith and Narrow didn't feel beholding to make him feel at home no more.

Now, this here Kay fellow had been scratching out a living putting together some of the best flocks of laying hens in the entire Rockies. But he had always been hankering for a excuse to get into dairy farming.

Once he heard that Giles was coming through looking for a new opportunity to get a milking contraption set up, Kay up and sold off his flocks of laying hens and told Giles he was ready to lay his entire life savings on the line for a dairy farm.

Now, not only was Kay a down right clever chicken farmer, but he and his wife Norma had come up with the idea about how to work at farming without experiencing one of the all time problems what most farmers had to put up with.

If you've ever lifted a pitch fork full of hay, or crawled under a chicken roost to get that last egg, or even squatted down beside old Bessie to get on with your milking, one of the most aggravating things what would happen is having what ever it is your working in, fall down the front of your britches. And then being so danged busy that you just put up with either that sprig of alfalfa, or dried up chicken dropping, or splat of cow leavings a working itself down the inside of your pant leg for the rest of the day.

One evening after having a handful of chicken mash working down his pant leg all day, Kay scrapes his boots off at the back door and came in for dinner. He sees Norma standing there fixing dinner with her everyday kitchen apron on.

Right then and there, he grabs her by the hand and drags her over to the sewing basket. He then tells her to take off that apron while he commences to pull of his britches. He then says, "Ma, I want you to cut that apron of yours right in half at the waste and then sew the top right on to these working britches of mine."

Well, this was just the beginning of what soon became your bib-overalls.

Before you knowed it, Norma was making them in fancy gray-striped denim. Farmers was coming a days ride just to get themselves a pair. Nothing was lost on this here bunch of paying customers neither. Being as clever as they was, Norma and Kay had ask who ever inquired for a pair, for what purpose they was a wanting them. Then if they was a carpenter, Norma would sew a nice wide loop on one side for hanging a hammer from and then one on the other for hanging whatever other tool was used most after the hammer.

If you said your was running a general store, she would sew long narrow pockets in the front for carrying pencils, and wide pockets in the middle for carrying your ciphering pad.

Why she even sewed up a pair for Mayor Bateman what had special pockets for carrying different kinds of seed what he peddled to make his regular livelihood. And that pair alone brought in hundreds of other orders just from Noal out visiting each day wearing his and telling folks about where he got them!

Kay hisself never went no where without wearing them and he even kept a fresh, clean pair ready for Sunday-go-to-meeting. Of course he would also wear hisself a right nice white starched shirt, high collar, dark tie and his Sunday-go-to meeting black coat. But honest Abe Lincoln hisself couldn't a looked more proper.

Anyway, this was quite a business and based on this here background of the Smith's being so successful, Giles agreed to go into partners for the building of the first milking contraption in Little Willow.

Narrow had left Giles behind to take on this here new venture a couple of weeks ago. By now, he and Port was about a day's ride North of their final destination with these pecan trees when their horses started doing a little more than their normal snorting, and started to lay their ears back like as there was something not yet seen what was in the wind.

Port looks over to Narrow and says, "Looks like we got ourselves some kind of storm brewing up and coming from the Northeast."

Narrow looks back over his left shoulder, and sure enough, there was a big black cloud moving toward them. He knowed right off that this wasn't no storm cloud. He'd seen something like this prêt near fifteen years back and he dreaded the thought a remembering what he was danged sure it was.

"Port," Narrow says, "Remember back about fifteen years ago? I was just knee-high to a grasshopper then, but we'd had our crops in about two months and the taters and grain was just started to bud out. When out of the Northeastern sky a cloud just like this one moved in. Folks started to cheering, figuring it was a long needed rain, only to find that it wasn't no rain at all. It ended up being crickets what swooped in and prêt near cleaned out every last crop until them gulls came in and started swallowing them up and then flying out to the lake where they spit them up and then they come on back for more."

Port swallows and says, "I remember it well. If this here is another one of them clouds, these pecan trees are going to be picked clean before we can get them under cover. Besides, they ain't no seagulls down here to eat these critters like what saved us last time."

Just in the matter of time it took for Port to say what he just said, that cloud moved in. Rather than try to run for cover, Narrow and port just sat there watching a miracle of nature like as most folks had never seen.

These wasn't no crickets, nor was they locusts nor hoppers neither. These was butterflies. Big as you please orange and blacks. They wasn't eating neither. They was just migrating like Northern geese.

Here was Narrow and Port sitting on the front of a bare Conestoga wagon load of pecan trees right smack in the middle of what must have been thousands of butterflies.

You wouldn't have believed it in a million years. These butterflies must have just been looking for a place to take themselves a rest, because they just lit themselves down right all over Narrow, Port and their wagon and hundreds of little trees.

Yes sir, there it was, a sight of nature happening in the middle of nowhere in particular. Thousands of butterflies just a roosting themselves like 'n entire coat of flapping back and orange all over this lonesome wagon and two sitting Cowboys.

It's times like these when a Cowboy kind of figures God Hisself just needs some entertaining. Just sitting up on some cloud somewhere, seeing what would happen if he had a whole mess a butterflies come to visit two human beings.

Port and Narrow didn't say nothing, and even the horses stopped fidgeting, snorting and swatting. Cowboys and horses a like, just being there, covered with slow flapping butterflies for what might be measured as a entire God's minute.

Then, as quick as they lit, they up and left. Not even taking nary a nibble from a single pecan leaf.

Narrow looks over at Port and says, "I expect this here is one of them times what keeps you from getting your hair cut ain't it."

Port just smiles and says, "Well, I've give up figuring. But that's as good a reason as any for keeping old Rex's barbering shears a working on somebody else. Let's get these nags a moving before we make this out to be some kind of spiritual experience."

Now being a Cowboy ain't generally figured to be a pretty job. But Narrow knew he'd just been paid a Cowboy's wages, what you can't spend at no saloon.

By sundown they was within sight of the tall red buttes they was a heading for and the sage had given way to more tumbleweed and bigger cactus. The sunset was reflecting off the wild morning glory that had long since closed up. A carpet of desert grass was enjoying the last of it's short life before the heat of summer would eventually kill it off.

And God was closing down another day on a Cowboy's trail.

CHAPTER 12

▼

HOP'N AND POKE'N

Humming birds are prêt near the most entertaining creatures what a relaxing Cowboy can observe.

Narrow had built a real nice humming bird feeder what he had up and give to Port for letting him bunk out at the Trading Post when he was betwixt Cowboy'n jobs.

He had come up with the idea of making a feeder by carving out a whole sugar beet. Then he would fill her up with spring water, and with the exception of refilling every week or so, depending on how many humming birds was feeding from it, this beet would give off sugar and continue to last throughout the entire summer.

Port and Narrow was now just sitting out on the porch visiting and watching two of these humming birds fight at each other over the sweet water what enticed them to stick their hollow beaks into the small feeder openings. These humming birds figured they both had squatting rights to this contraption and around sunset every night they would come buzzing in to get their drinks, and then commence to spend more time fending off each other, than actually getting their beaks filled.

While Narrow and Port was sitting there watching them humming birds making surprise attacks at each other, coming around the corner of the porch, or buzzing in from around the side of the rain barrel, they hear the familiar sound of old Doc Sorenson's buckboard clacking down through the cottonwoods.

This wasn't too unusual because Doc stopped by prêt near twice a week to pick up doctoring supplies that Port would order for him. This being because they was too fragile to come in through the regular mail, and had to be brung in on supply wagons. Least wise that's what the Doc told most folks as to why he had to go to Port's. Truth be known, he generally just needed a fresh supply of drinking liquor and beings Port's was the only place to get any, he'd just arranged with Port to be a dropping off point for his doctoring supplies.

Anyway, Doc wasn't alone this time. He had hisself a passenger sitting there beside him on the buckboard seat. Doc introduced this passenger as a feller by the name of M. Dayton. And further explained that he was going to break this young sawbones in as what was to be the new Doc for Little Willow and surrounding parts.

Seems that Doc Sorenson here had got hisself so busy performing birthings for these big Mormon families that he just plumb ran out of time to do your ordinary doctoring.

This here Doc Dayton fellow had finished all the book learning folks had to offer up in Wyoming where he had been brung up. So he had came on down to the Great Basin to learn about doctoring from Doc Sorensen hisself.

According to the Doc, he'd also been spending some time over at Rex's barbering shop, learning about pulling of teeth and doctoring feet for your every day corns and calluses what Rex would usually cut off for you if you paid him 'n extra two bits when you was getting your hair cut.

Well, no sooner did this young Doc Dayton open his mouth than both Narrow and Port knowed he was a right smart fellow. Why he spewed out words explaining about parts of human beings bodies the likes of which neither of these Cowboys never heard before.

He started explaining about your ectomys and octomys, and is-a-ments and ain't-a-ments. And then before they knowed it he had these sorry buckaroos striped down to nothing but their long handled underwear and boots, and commences to giving them what he calls a physical examination.

He's then got them hopping and turning, and coughing on purpose. Then he tells them to drop their back door trap and bend over for some further examining.

Well, up to this point, things was entertaining enough to just go along with him. But when it comes to dropping your back door trap for some young saw bones what has got hisself all kinds of poking instruments ready for poking…this here's where a Cowboy draws the line.

Both Narrow and Port starts to telling this Doc Dayton that they is much appreciating for what been physical examined already. They would just be letting him know if they ever had no noticeable ailing in them parts what he ain't looked at nor poked through their back door trap for to examine.

He was right respectful of their wishes of not being poked no more, and packs up his doctoring bag while Narrow and Port gets their britches back on.

While all this physical examining was going on Doc Sorenson had managed to sneak his new supply of drinking liquor from Port's cellar without Doc Dayton seeing him. Turns out that Doc Dayton was also a might religious and Doc Sorenson had to take care that he didn't make his drinking habit knowed. After all, he wasn't about to expose hisself to getting no religion at his age and with his satisfying vices.

Well, that exciting part of the day being over, Narrow tells Port that he best be getting back to work if he was going to be ready for the deer hunting and horse breaking trip he'd been invited to.

By the next morning Narrow had rode his horse Kant about twenty miles South to rendezvous with a close friend of his by the name of L. Mendenhall. Lynn had hisself the unusual job of supervising the digging of canals to bring down mountain lake water to the new valley farms what was being started up.

From time to time he'd ask Narrow to come down and help him get some of the new horses broke for his working crew and also to get the ones what was already broke shoed for the winter.

The problem was that Lynn wasn't given no kind of extra money to buy hisself no decent horseflesh and as a result he had hisself the most sorry string of riding animals what ever been saddled. Usually he ended up buying them from a slaughterhouse that had taken them in for glue rendering.

Name of the owner of this here slaughterhouse was Kentucky Martinez. Later in life he got out of slaughtering and got into the general store business. But for now he'd shortened his name up a might for branding purposed and branded all these nags with the abbreviation of K for Kentucky and Mart for Martinez, this coming out as "K-Mart" on the branding iron.

Anyway, one of these K-Mart nags had the name of "Ignorant". Now this here horse didn't even have what you called your ordinary horse sense. He was just as ignorant as his name implied. What ever it was you wanted him to do, he'd just up and do the opposite. Like if you was wanting to check his left front hoof and started tugging on his hawk, he'd just lift up his right front hoof. Then when you went around to check out that one he'd been holding up, he'd just put it down and lift up the other one.

Well, the boys had learned to rein him right if they wanted to go left and vice versa and just made sure they wasn't standing behind him when somebody was trying to get his mouth open to take a bridle bit.

Then there was Nebo the Mountain Horse. Kind of a long name for a mount, but he deserved it. Nebo the Mountain Horse had been gilded when he was about seven years old, and that being about five years too late he'd taken it quite personal.

Unlike Ignorant, this was one smart critter. Leaving the barn you might figure you had yourself the best horse what ever been rode. Why he'd take mountain trails like he was some kind of billygoat, drink when you took him to water, stand still when you was shooting from his back, and not even spook when you had to load a fresh shot deer on his backside.

But when the day was over and his rider was figuring to turn him around and head for home, that's when he'd get his revenge on 'n otherwise unsuspecting Cowboy, for that late castration what he'd received. Seems as soon as he had a sense for it being time to head for home, he'd just break into a flat out run. It wouldn't make no difference if he and his rider was in thick quakies, heavy pines, low mountain scrub oak or even picking themselves down a steep rocky slope. He'd just run all the way back to the barn and there wasn't no sense trying to stop him. The best advice was just to try to hang on until he got you home.

He left many a Cowboy with a long walk home who just couldn't hang on for the entire trip back or got swiped off by a low hanging branch. But that was just his way and the boys seemed to live with it.

Then there was a nag by the name of Lightening. Unlike the other ponies what was rode by who ever showed up that day, Lightening was only rode by Lynn's twin sons. One being named Tim and the other being named Terry. Well, these twins was identical and to add to the confusion their Pa, Lynn hisself, couldn't tell them apart neither. But that's a whole other story.

These two boys was notorious for sneaking off during the day to take themselves a daytime nap. And they took turns on old Lightening depending on which one of them was about to be the most lazy. You see Lightening got his name on account of he was just the opposite of lightening. This horse was slow and lazy. Why he was one of the few horses what ever been born what had a hankering for taking daytime snoozes. And unlike other horses what did all their sleeping standing up, this here nag would lay hisself down like a human being and just snore up 'n afternoon of dreaming about what ever it was horses dreamed.

The boys would be on a long ride, or out moving sheep around to help graze down the canal banks and for you knowed it Lightening and whichever one of the twins was riding him would be off sleeping in the shade of some stand of pines.

It also turned out that neither Lynn nor any of the other men could get this lazy hunk of horseflesh to move faster than a walk when he wasn't laying on his side somewhere a snoring away another siesta.

To make a long story short, the first thing Lynn was asking of Narrow on this trip was to get Lightening trained for respectable work like the rest of the nags, or he was just going to send him back to the K-Mart slaughtering house.

Now Narrow wasn't one for spurring horses, but it wouldn't of mattered in this case because Lightening had hisself double growed calluses where Cowboys had been trying to spur him for years. So no spurs used by Narrow was going to do no good no how. But he decides to get hisself a nice stiff willow branch and sharpens one end. He then climbs up on Lightening and without saying his first giddy-up, he commences to prodding Lightenings behind for a spot what might be tender enough to get the message through.

Well, Lightening just stands there with his head leaning down forward like usual. His front legs crossed, one of his back legs leaning against the other one and his eyes kind of half shut...looking like they is about to close permanent for another daytime dozing.

At first it seemed that this idea wasn't no good neither. But then Narrow tries a nice hard poke right at the top of where Lightening's tail is coming out from. Well, this here Cowboy is here to tell you it was like God Hisself had touched that horse with a lightening bolt for which he should have been named. He picks up his head, perks up his ears, opens his eyes to a point like they never been opened before and commences to prancing around like as he has just been made honorary horse Marshall of the Pioneer Day's Parade.

Well, that Cowboy'n job being done, once again Narrow remembers that Cowboy'n is a profession what ain't appreciated for its value unless you been one. And no amount of physical examinations, nor ectomys, nor octomys, nor is-a-ments, nor ain't-a-ments can put no Cowboy in you if you ain't one. Nor take no Cowboy out of you if you is one.

CHAPTER 13

▼

CLUCK'N AND DUCK'N

Around mid-October of every year the high mountain quakies turn themselves into every kind of yellow and gold that a Cowboy can imagine. This year wasn't no different. Narrow and the Mendenhalls, including Lynn, his oldest son Johnny and his twin sons Tim and Terry was all finished getting the riding stock prepared for winter. Like in years past they was rewarding themselves with a week or two of high mountain deer hunting.

The early snows usually started moving the deer down from the pines to look for forage in the meadows. For the most part, both the bucks and does was fattened up for the cold weather to come, but they wasn't going to miss no extra meals if they could help it.

Narrow hisself wasn't much of a venison lover, and didn't much care for shooting down deer just for the sport of it. But this here hunt was kind of traditional and he'd missed out last year when he was up the Yellowstone swimming in mud pots and poaching salmon in them boiling geysers. So he was down right happy to be here with his good friends.

It was their first day out and like on the first day out on past hunts they was just kind of poking around, trying to figure where they eventually wanted to hunt the rest of the week. They also was yet to shoot down their evening meal. This was somewhat a worry to Narrow because it was getting on to late afternoon and the first day of the hunt it was always agreed that supper would be fresh shot pine hen.

Ordinarily this ain't no problem, because every Cowboy knowed that your pine hen is the second most stupid bird what ever growed feathers. The first most stupid bird, being your ordinary, barnyard variety, of laying hen. Not only is your laying hen born stupid, but they continues being stupid even after they ain't living no more.

Narrow knew this from first hand experience being that when he was just a youngster, about twice a month he and the rest of his family would get themselves invited over to the Smiths for a chicken supper.

This usually happened on a Sunday afternoon and commenced right after noon chores. You see it wasn't just supper that was involved, it took prêt near every member of both families to get things ready. This is when he learned hisself about the stupidity of chickens.

First, he and the other young'ns was sent out to catch the chicken what was to be cooked for dinner. You would think if you had yourself a yard full of chickens you would just catch yourself whichever one you catches first, then be done with it. But chicken farming wasn't that simple. It was always a particular chicken what had to be caught. Somehow it was knowed that this particular chicken wasn't laying her share of eggs and rather than let her peck up good feed what was broadcast for regular egg laying chickens, she was now meant to be Sunday supper.

Now, chicken catching is one of your first lessons of eventually being a growed up Cowboy. If you can barehanded catch yourself a chicken when you're still wet behind the ears, then later in life learning to punch cattle from horseback comes a might easier.

Narrow and the other young'ns knowed that if you was fixing to catch yourself a chicken, the smartest thing to do is wait until the middle of the night and then just go pluck them off their roosts while they is sleeping. But this not being the dark of night, these young'ns just had to do her the hard way.

Now chickens got their eyes on the side of their heads. So they can't see straight ahead and they're too stupid to look back. But if you run at them head on, they usually just fly straight up in your face. If you comes up on them from one side or the other they can see you. But then they end up running circles around you so they can keep seeing you from which ever eye it is, what is on the side of the head what is looking at you.

This leaves your sneaking up from behind. Now sneaking up on a spooked chicken is about as easy as trying to stay awake while your sleeping to see if you can hear yourself snore. And about as smart too.

See, since your chickens are so dumb they can't never figure themselves which way they is going to run...they ain't no way for a thinking human being to figure it out neither.

In spite of all this running around, trying to out-stupid what can't never be out-stupid-ed, eventually Narrow or one of the other couple dozen young'ns, by accident, falls on the right bird and brings her over to the chopping stump for the next part of the chicken's stupidity.

Kay had been waiting there having just sharpened up his hatchet. Then for this part Narrow's Ma would take the youngest kids inside. But for the older boys this was where they got their first experiences of roping.

Narrow's Pa would pass out roping lariats to Narrow and the other boys and say, "Get yourselves ready. Which ever of you gets a lasso around this bird gets the gizzard."

No sooner was the "Get ready to win your gizzard" speech over, than Kay brings that hatchet down hard chopping of that chicken's head, than it commences to running throughout the entire barnyard while her heads still laying back on the chopping stump.

Ropes are twirling and missing everywhere and loops are falling in places that bird ain't even headed for. But eventually a rope would get caught, by accident, around one of the feet and the hen would be dragged in to be properly plucked and prepared for supper.

Narrow kind of thought back on these experiences as he and Lynn was sitting beneath a pine tree with their six shooters drawn, waiting for a pine hen they had spotted, to come clucking around for a open shot. Just about this time, they hear about half a dozen head of deer come crashing through the quakies behind them. No sooner could they get themselves turned around than they hear gun fire coming at them, like as they was sitting with Sam Houston hisself down at the Alamo.

Then they see Johnny, Tim and Terry come riding behind from where there is deer coming from, unloading their repeating rifles right at the deer, not knowing who it is what is on the other side.

About this time, Narrow and Lynn figures that this pine hen ain't about to be the only one what was to be shot and they dive for underneath and behind this big old pine and start shooting over their heads. Tim, Terry and Johnny hear the shooting but figures it's a coming from other hunters, and not to be out shot, they proceeds to emptying every last what shell they got left in their deer rifles, aiming through this big pine towards where it is them deer went.

Well, that old pine hen had had enough and flushes out of this pine tree right as Johnny comes riding up. This causing old Ignorant on which Johnny is riding, to rare back and dumps Johnny right at the base of the tree, where he then looks up to find hisself staring up the barrels of two six shooters held by two old Cowboys what was about ready to defend themselves against their own flesh and blood.

While Johnny's still sitting there with his mouth wide open and his hands raised up, Tim comes riding up on Lightening and then Nebo goes by heading back for home with Terry following close behind on foot.

Lynn and Narrow admitted to the boys that they hadn't never figured they would be shooting their own flesh and blood. But if worse came to worse, and the shooting got closer, in order to save their sorry skins, they had decided to send them horses what these boys was riding, to the happy horse meadows in the sky. Least wise that's what they figured might get the shooting to stop.

In spite of all this excitement, and to once again confirm the stupidity of your pine hens, that same pine hen came clucking right back at this bunch of (sorry about it but we almost killed each other) Cowboys.

We was pretty much out of shooting lead, but with the one bullet he had left, It goes without saying that Lynn put this hen out of her stupid misery with one shot and turned to the boys and said, "I don't know about Narrow here, but I think it only right that you boys do the plucking and cooking. Besides, I've got some britches what need changing."

Much to Narrow's pleasure, them was the last deer what was seen all week. And for his way of thinking the best deer hunts was them what only put a stupid pine hen or two out of their miseries.

This last week had brought down the first good snowfall and by now them golden quakies leaves was prêt near gone for the season. Narrow had decided to try and keep his promise from last year to meet old friends up in Wyoming. So he said his goodbyes to Lynn and the boys and headed out alone for a long Cowboy ride north.

CHAPTER 14

▼

COWBOY'S FEARS

If they had their druthers, most Cowboys would follow the geese and buffalo each winter to the deserts of Mexico. Narrow wasn't no different, but in spite of his druthers, this winter he'd found hisself in a might sorry set of circumstances.

There's only about two things a Cowboy fears having to face. One is having to put a good horse down due to some trail injury what might just get healed up if you was back home for doctoring and pasturing. And the second being, what to do when faced with the prospect of being around women.

Generally speaking, most Cowboys had themselves a Ma somewhere. And for some part of their lives they might of even been raised with sisters or other female kin. But when it came to associating with non-related women folk, Cowboys was about as skillful as a earthworm trying to mate with a diamondback rattler. Like that earthworm, they like what they sees, but don't have no idea what they'd be in for if they got close enough to find out.

For most Cowboys, their only experiences with women was what little womanizing they might get at some sorry saloon, or being introduced to some trapper's squaw what still only speaks Injun and keeps her head down when men is present.

Truth be known, there just wasn't no good reason for no other kind of women to be taken themselves out West of the Missouri no how, unless they was married to some sorry pioneer, who had them expecting their tenth or eleventh young'n. And given the choice of going with him or staying back in Missouri to fend for themselves, they'd choose to go with him just in case they was lucky enough to see him killed from his own stupidity of trying to drag a wagon load of kin to some place nobody knew what it'd be!

He didn't know why, but while Narrow was sitting there staring at them big brown eyes of this pack pony, what he figured he'd have to put out of her misery, Narrow commenced to thinking on what few women he'd been introduced to.

First one he remembers was a woman what his scout Howdy was courting. He can't remember her name for sure, but it might have been Doris or some other frilly name like that.

What brung her West was her strange doctoring ability. Of course she wasn't no regular doctor, and couldn't pull no teeth nor cut hair for that matter. It's just that she'd come up with ways of taking care of things what is ailing folks what don't make no sense. Except for if you is the one what is ailing and what she just done for you solves your problem or gives you some relief.

Like if you was choking on something being stuck in your windpipe. Instead of thumping you on your back, or having a couple of other Cowboys grabbing you by your spurs and dangling you out the upstairs window, she'd just stand you up leaning your back against a solid post, have you shut your eyes and open your mouth. And then without no warning give you a sharp elbow right under your ribs, upstream of your breadbasket. And then what ever it was stuck would come shooting out right at her splttoon for which she was aiming you. Then to make sure you wouldn't be having this problem again, she'd give you a thimble full of some vile tasting concoction made of tiny green oranges and say to you "you just been healed by the use of the lime lick method."

Well, she would also stick a needle twixt your toes for curing of headaches, fill your belly button with salt for toothaches, have you suck on a piece of heifer hoof for in-growed toenails and have you wear a gaggle of garlic and onions around your neck for getting rid of your everyday green apple quick trots.

Now, all this doctoring ability aside, she was quite a gal and had herself a real nice set of ankles to beat. But of course she was spoken for by Howdy and Narrow had been respectful about not showing no interest.

He also had been given the privilege of meeting his other wintering partner, Jay's wife to be. Jay had been busy planting and raising them big spuds up North of Bear Lake area. But had hisself all planned to be marrying a young gal by the name a Joanne.

Now this Joanne had it in her mind, that whoever it was, was going to be her husband, wasn't going to be no farmer. And no tater farmer for that matter. She had it in her mind that there ought to be some husband smart enough what would figure out a way of inventing flying contraptions. That is so folks wouldn't have to ride in no covered wagons, buckboards, stagecoaches or no trains for that matter. And if he done it, folks would pay top dollar for a ride in these contraptions and the end result would make them both richer than if they struck gold.

Now it ain't no Cowboy's place to tell no other Cowboy what kind of women it is he should ought to be courting. But seeing one of your feller buckaroos ready to get hitched up to someone what is suffering from the ill effects of smoking loco weed, when they hadn't even been smoking none, was almost more than a Cowboy could take.

This here Joanne was a real looker, and loco or not, given the opportunity of leaving your boots by her bed at night might just keep you trying to hammer wings on your buckboard. So Narrow and the other boys weren't about to blame Jay for trying to please this gal even though she was crazier than a hoot owl what got his head stuck backwards.

Then Narrow remembers the last time he was back in his hometown of Little Willow. He'd had hisself introduced to the new school marm what had been brung in since that Washburn feller had died out a being scared to death from what he thought was seeing a Injun.

Well, being a school marm, as such, she wasn't introduced with no first name, but just referred to as Miss Boulter.

Now she had herself the darkest hair and eyes as what Narrow had ever seen in a non-Injun. And she looked just like one of them cameo pictures what hung in ladies hat shop windows.

But these good looks wasn't the only thing for which she was knowed for. Seems she come up with ways of conducting book learning that got your reading, writing and ciphering done without your even knowing you was been exposed to no educating. One of the ways she'd get this done was by having the church piano moved over to the school house during the week for school days and then she'd bring in a friend of hers by the name of Miss Mary for the playing of it.

Seems this Miss Mary was called by her given name because her proper name was too danged hard to say for your not yet educated kids. But anyways, she had herself a real music playing ability and since there wasn't no saloons in Little Willow for your playing during the week, she made herself available to this Miss Boulter.

They'd get those young'ns singing songs what had book learning built right in. Why they had them ciphering how many animals it was Old McDonald had on his farm, how little, Little Mary's little lamb was, and for smarter students they was teaching, they even had them learning non-English a singing "nick-nack-paddy-wack" and other high flouting ways of speaking, what a Cowboy couldn't even remember, let alone explain to no other Cowboy.

For a Cowboy like Narrow, even as clever as he is, all he was able to say when introduced to this Miss Boulter was, "Pleasure to make your acquaintance, Miss…", and then he proceeded to forget her name and just kind of looked down and turned his hat around in his hands like as he might drop it if he didn't. And then he did anyway.

Well, by the time he looked up from picking up his hat, she had high tailed it on over to ring her come-on-back-from-recess bell, and that had been the end of his proper introduction.

Now, these was three mighty interesting women what wasn't related to him, wasn't your easy women, and wasn't no squaws neither. What he'd learned about women from them was that he hadn't learned nothing that would make no difference about what he knew about women the next time he'd have the pleasure of meeting one.

All this thinking on the second most fearful thing of what a Cowboy has to face has got Narrow to figure that maybe facing the prospect of meeting women is really the first most fearful thing what a Cowboy has to face. He decides that this horse's leg could be splinted, and if rested proper, maybe even healed by spring.

Narrow had found hisself in high snow country with a lame horse. But had plenty of dry powder for hunting, a nice cave opening for taking shelter and doctoring this pack pony, and most important, no real fears what he hadn't already given a long Cowboy's thought to.

CHAPTER 15

▼

ALMOST DEAD

Narrow was almost dead.

The sad part of it was that he knowed he was almost dead.

He had been laying there face down a sucking up desert sand for prêt near three days now, ever since he'd been ambushed by a couple of outlaws what must of figured he was carrying gold in his saddlebags.

They shot him in the leg right close to them parts what a Cowboy never wants to get shot at. Then danged if it didn't ricochet on over to the other leg and left him with no way of walking. They had also taken his horse and his pack pony and pretty much left him for dead.

He weren't right sure if he hadn't of died already and come back as some kind of sorry sidewinder what just couldn't figure out how to side wind.

But laying there with nothing to do but lay in this desert and prêt near freeze to death at night and frying hisself during the day, gave him time to think on some of the folks what he'd come to know over his short life. This here prêt near dyin' had caused him to remember a Cowboy what had told him how he hisself had almost died once.

This Cowboy's name was O. Pierce, and he had hisself a mighty unusual way of speaking. It wasn't that he said his words funny or nothing like that. It was just that every thing he finished saying ended up sounding a whole lot like what it was he'd just said before. Kind of like your singing except for there wasn't no tune involved.

Narrow commenced to remembering what it was this Cowboy had told he and some of the other boys what was hanging around Rex's barbering shop one day on the subject of he himself almost dieing. To the best of his recollection it went something like this:

"Boys'" he said:

"When your hands are tied behind you,
With some slowly tightening leather,
And your dangling from your boots,
A swinging upside down all tethered.

And the hair you used to have on top,
Between your ears and beneath your hat,
Is now the prize of some young brave
And hanging from his belt is where it's at.

And as you're peering up between your boots,
You see the turkey buzzards flying,
Aiming circles around the desert sky,
Licking hungry beaks for a Cowboy frying.

And you hears yourself the slithering hiss
Of a slowly approaching rattler,
That ain't never seen such a sorry sight
As a Cowboy's face getting bloated and fatter.

You start to think why it was you decided
To be a growed up Cowboy for a living.

Seems that back when all you knew about
What they done, was roping and brand giving.

There weren't no way you figured being part of,
What you was preparing yourself to become,
Was no kind of upside down, hanging, starving,
Miserable Cowboy, enjoying the setting sun.

Well, one thing about that Otis, he always seemed to end his stories on a high note, even if it didn't make no sense to do so. But this here ability of his to rhyme these sentences together weren't necessarily respectful as to if the result came out truthful or not neither.

About this time of Narrow's suffering he starts to remembering how he and the other cowpunchers would plant herbs, taters, carrots and other of your hardier food stuffs along the trail for when they returned or if another drive was to come along and be in need. They usually marked these what they called "stashes" with a burial cross, and then they'd do a carving of something like "Mr. Herb RIP", right on that cross.

This here proved as a good mark because your Injuns knowed what a wood cross-meant and out of respect for the buried dead, be they whites or reds, they'd take themselves a wide berth around these crosses.

The Cowboys what could read knowed right off that if it said Mr. Herb they could start rooting around for them herbs what was most likely planted near by, and didn't have to take to worry about clanking their shovels into no dead bodies.

Well, where he was a laying, being not too far off a well used cattle drive trail, he decided that if he can get hisself up on a nearby rock, maybe he can spot hisself a tombstone of old Mr Herb, and maybe root up enough vittles to keep hisself alive for another day or two.

Now in the process of trying to pull his sorry bones up on this rock, by accident what is left of his chaps and pant leg flops open and he gets his first good look at his wounds. Now this here part's hard to explain. Except for if you been hanging around preachers or other God fearing men.

Seems most of what discomfort he was suffering from wasn't from the gunshot wound, but what was now a whole danged army of red ants what had chewed them wounds right together. And was now retreating down off that pant leg with about forty of them carrying that danged colt slug over their heads like as they was the Children of Israel a bringing that gold calf off to some mountain for worshipping.

Narrow just sat there and watched until the last ant picked his way down over what was left of a broken spur a dangling off his dust-covered boot. Then he commenced to speculate on how it was that he'd plumb forgot about how thirsty he'd been while watching these varmints a marching off like they'd just been called back due to some kind of direct orders.

About this time Narrow starts to notice that this here rock is getting a might harder to hang on to. And it ain't because it's slippery neither!

Danged if the cactus didn't start to sway, and then the whole dad-burned desert started to roll like as this here sand just turned itself into the Great Salt Lake itself.

Well, for he knowed it, the ground split wide open, and fresh water was a spraying up like them Yellowstone geysers. By the time things settled down, Narrow found hisself setting next to a full spring of water, fit for drinking and bathing, both of which he commenced to do right quick as to avoid it leaving before he woke up from what he figured was nothing but a Cowboy's desert dream. He'd heard of earthquakes, but never figured he experience one, nor have his life saved as a result. But he did, and he was.

No sooner did he get his whistle good and wet, and his clothes all washed, and a nice Cowboy bathing over with in this God-given usher, than he hears the rumbling of on-coming cattle. Sure enough there comes 'n entire herd of water sniffing cattle at a full stampede with his own mount Kant, and his pack pony moving right long side. Just as if Narrow was in the saddle hisself and heading that herd to their next drink.

It didn't take Narrow no more than a couple of days to get that herd all watered and grazed and then he turned them Northeast for 'n end-of-summer drive back to the Great Basin, thinking all along, that in spite of the fact that he'd been almost dead, there must be some reason for him not yet heading for Cowboy heaven.

He also started speculating on if he would have been heaven-bound anyhow. And decided right there, that once back home, he best have a long talk with Port, and find out if maybe he ought to make his Ma happy and possibly show up at church just to see what might be learnt.

After all, he weren't getting no younger. And maybe he best get acquainted with his maker before he goes on to meet him on a permanent basis.

CHAPTER 16

▼

SITTING HOME FOR CHRISTMAS

The winds was howling down every canyon in the Wasatch front and Little Willow was getting its share from Bear Canyon and Rocky Mouth. The snow was drifted up prêt near twelve feet high on the North and East corners of Narrow's place, and long, thick icicles had formed on the West and South corners.

But the cold outside only made the warmth inside more appreciated.

This Christmas Eve Narrow was sitting in one of the two oak rockers he and his bride was give for their wedding, which they'd had a year ago last spring. Yep, Narrow had up and got hisself hitched to that school Marm, Miss Boulter, on account of he couldn't stop thinking about them big brown eyes, nor that dark hair of hers neither.

'Course, Miss Boulter had been walking around with a sparkle in her eye since they was first introduced back at the school ground. Seems all her high fluting education, what prepared her for her school marming, went clean out the window when it came to Narrow. He was just about the best Cowboy and blacksmith West of Abilene, and could fashion or fix prêt near everything what got broke or needed inventing. But in spite of this, he was just a Cowboy, and Cowboy'n wasn't no life for no kind of school Marm to marry in to.

The plumb loco nature of human beings falling in love was the only thing to answer for it. And Narrow swallowed hard and said "Yup" when Bishop Adamson pronounced the nuptials.

Miss Boutler had agreed to allow Narrow to go on one Cowboy'n assignment each year, but the rest of the time he had agreed to stay right home in Little Willow and tend to blacksmithing at his Pa's. This kept him busy enough, but he was also working as much as possible on his own business of doing fancy whittling and woodworking. In addition to fashioning your pantry cabinets, bedroom drawers, and other kinds of desks and in-house furniture, he was commencing to making hisself downright famous with his ability to whittle and carve some of the most easy sitting out-house seats what a human being ever sat on.

The secret to this, was his ability to take a look at your backside, and without no measurements, nor scientific ciphering, nor a making you drop your britches neither, he'd go on back to his wood shop and between fashioning and carving, come up with a seat what was so danged comfy he had folks coming from as far North as Cache Valley and as far South as St. George, to get themselves one of his custom commode seats.

He even was getting compliments from the women folk who for years had been complaining that their men had been building commode seats what just wasn't a comfort to a woman.

Of course, Narrow had to be real careful when it came to making these seats for women on account of he had to look at their behinds for the measuring. But he couldn't be a looking for no other reasons at the same time.

Now this was even more difficult with them women what wore them big bustles. But he kind of had a way to cipher what took these things into account. As far as he knew it, he hadn't had a sorry customer yet. That is except for some of the local wives what was complaining that their husbands had been slacking off work due to the fact that they was spending so much time in the cranny, only coming out to say it was the most comfortable place they had sat in their entire life.

About a month back, Brother Brigham hisself had been down to see Narrow and had been so happy with the seat Narrow had fashioned for him, he had up and give him a contract to fashion a seat for each one of his wives for their Christmas presents. Seems Narrow had also come up with the clever idea of making them portable so each person could have their own...they could just slide a Narrow custom-fit commode seat on over the commode port in the outhouse when they was wanting to use it just for themselves.

Well, this here new job of making this big order for Brother Brigham was quite a challenge, what with only getting but one good look at all forty-eight wives without them knowing what he was looking for, and all on the same day. And then trying to remember what it was he had to remember right in time for making each seat.

But, Narrow had finished the job just two days before Christmas and borrowed Doc Sorenson's buckboard for delivering them.

Brother Brigham was downright pleased and paid him in hard coin. Then, after taking a trial sit hisself, he pulled Narrow into his office and told him that come spring he wanted to talk to him about accepting the general contract of fashioning commode seats for the Salt Lake City Temple, what was now being built. But he also shook a plump finger at Narrow and told him he better get his life in order, because he couldn't go awarding no contracts even for commode seats to no one what didn't show up to church on a regular basis.

Well, Narrow had been thinking on church anyway and pretty much resolved hisself to being a Sunday attender, come good weather.

Anyway, here he was on Christmas Eve, just two days after delivering four dozen commode seats to Brother Brigham a rocking in one of these oak rockers and holding his new baby son what had been born just a couple of months back on a warm fall day in October.

Narrow wasn't home for the birthing because he'd been on the annual deer hunt at the time. Now it wasn't that he didn't want to be home for the birthing, but he'd shot hisself one of the biggest bucks what had ever been shot in them parts. Shot that eight point smack on the last day of the hunt. So it took Narrow and the boys a extra day to bring it out due to the fact that they had to give up their riding horses for carrying the meat.

By the time Narrow had come galloping home, both Doc Sorenson and Doc Dayton had left. This on account of two reasons. First being that the birthing was done and they really wasn't needed no more, and second being that they didn't want to be in shouting distance when Narrow showed up because Narrow's wife (and the mother of his new son) was madder than a preacher's wife whose young'n had just busted in on the annual ladies quilting bee carrying a armful of baby skunks.

She was mad and rightly so, on account of the fact that the birthing hadn't been a easy one. Both Docs had to use every bit of book learning and fancy doctoring what they had ever learned. And Narrow hadn't been there for none of the petticoat ripping ner hot water boiling neither. (Not to mention the hand wringing of the neighbor ladies due to the screaming of the mother.)

Well, it ain't quite polite to tell you right here what it was that Narrow's wife had to tell him when he did show up. But he ended up giving this first son of theirs, Buster. Being that his birth had nearly busted up his own parent's marriage.

Going on two months had past since Buster was born, and what with Narrows success with the commode seat business, Narrow's wife had pretty much got over her fretting from the birthing and they were both settled in for their first Christmas with their new born baby.

Besides, they both knew that on this Christmas morning, Narrow had carved up a gift for his wife what was just as good as any of what forty-eight wives of Brother Brigham hisself was unwrapping and trying out this very night.

Epilogue

▼

Narrow had himself many adventures what ain't told in this here book and continues living hisself a good and respectful life. Fact is, folks tell us that he's turned hisself into one of them what they call snowbirds. Living down in the Southern part of Utah in the winter time where them pecan trees have grown tall and true, just like his first son and other children that followed. Then, come spring, he migrates with the other birds back North, bringing his bride of over fifty years along and always with a gaggle a grand kids and great grand kids string'n behind just for the excitement of what may happen next.

About the Author

James R. "Buster" Thompson

Jim (he dropped the nickname of Buster when a teenager) is an off-spring of the West with a rich family heritage of pioneers, settlers, blacksmiths and Cowboys. He draws on family legends and traditional values for most of his writings.

He also credits his yearnings for the Old West on the fact that he has lived on the East Coast for the past thirty years. As a traveling executive he has also come to recognize the unique character of the Utah Cowboy. This includes the language of the mountain West which presents a challenge to write (and read), but is unequaled in embracing the richness of a culture that can only be described in double negatives, conjugational anomalies and recurring colloquialisms.

This writing style has provided Jim with a recreational diversion from his professional duties, which don't allow for no writing like what is in this here book.

0-595-31096-6